P9-CKL-611

DATE DUE

LUMP IT
—OR
LEAVE IT

Lump it
or
Leave it

FLORENCE
KING

ST. MARTIN'S
PRESS
NEW YORK

Library of Congress Cataloging-in-Publication Data

King, Florence.
    Lump it or leave it / Florence King.
       p.   cm.
    ISBN 0-312–04343–0
    I. Title.
    PS3561.I4754L8 1990
    814'.54—dc20
                               89–77920

First Edition
10 9 8 7 6 5 4 3 2 1

To the memory of my grandmother,
Lura Upton Ruding

CONTENTS

AUTHOR'S NOTE

I was going to call this new volume of anti-Americana *Tired, Poor, Huddled and Here.* The phrase popped into my head about ten years ago and I have been saving it for a title ever since. It wasn't really a good title because it suggests the immigrant experience, which is not the subject of this book. Nonetheless, I had my heart set on using it until something happened that made me change my mind.

I did not tour my last book, *Reflections in a Jaundiced Eye,* for two reasons. First, I hate to travel. Second, *Reflections* contained a section about how much I hate book tours and why, so St. Martin's could not very well ask the same people to schedule me after what I said about them. (I wrote the book-tour section to get out of touring and it worked!)

Since I had confined most of my shafts to television, St. Martin's arranged a stay-at-home tour consisting of newspaper interviews by people who came to me, and radio interviews via telephone.

Everything went well until I got into a fight with a snide yuppie radio host who tried to do the hard-hitting reporter number on me.

I blew up. "Listen, boy, stop playing Dan Rather with me or I'll hang up this damn telephone!"

"Well, what do you say to people who disagree with your opinions?"

"Like it or lump it!"

There was my title. My agent and my editor both loved it, so we were all set to go with it when something else happened.

St. Martin's publicity director Maryanne Mazzola has dozens of titles to remember. Maybe she had an unusually busy day, or maybe *Like It Or Lump It* underwent the same sea change as office gossip—*e.g.*, I did *not* pull a .38 on that copyeditor, it was a .22. In any event, Maryanne wrote me a note saying "I can't wait to read *Lump It Or Leave It*."

I saw at once that it was much better. It is less irascible, thus insuring that my national reputation for caring 'n' compassion will remain intact. It is a clever send-up of the right-wing bumper sticker, and most important of all, it expresses the only choice I have in a world that has been completely Americanized. In short, it's a perfect title, and I owe it to Maryanne Mazzola.

So let's hear it for Italians! They discover the damnedest things.

FIFTYSOMETHING

Lear's is the magazine "For The Woman Who Wasn't Born Yesterday."

Shakespearean buffs who think it is named for the Lear who said, "Let it stamp wrinkles in her brow of youth, with cadent tears fret channels in her cheeks," must think again. *Lear's* is the brainchild of sixtyish Frances Lear, the former Mrs. Norman Lear, who decided to build the confidence of older women by giving them their own magazine and naming it after the man who paid her $112 million for divorcing him.

Considering the way they edited my copy, they ought to call themselves *The Battle-Ax*. As far as I can tell, they do nothing for older women unless you want to count the ten years they took off my life.

Writing for women's magazines is a matter of skirting their various taboos. Pedophobia at *Family Circle* and Lesbianism at *Cosmopolitan* make sense, but the great taboo at *Lear's*, according to one of their many former editors, is the word *menopause*.

A shame, because I would have loved to write an article on it for them.

My thoughts on the menopause do not go over well with the kind of middle-aged women who say, "You're only as old as you feel," and then give a pert toss of the head. These are the women who buy the most surgical collars. They are also the women who buy the most plastic surgery; I have a professional acquaintance whose recent eyelid job has left her with a permanent expression of such poleaxed astonishment that she looks at all times as if she had just read one of my books.

About the most these women will say on the forbidden subject is a wistful murmur of "I miss my periods." If you reply, as I did, "That's like missing the Spanish Inquisition," your name will be entered in the *Index of Insensitivity* under Twatist. Between the upbeat seventies' psychobabble about "passages" and feminism's attempt to reduce menopause to a sheaf of mendacious stereotypes invented by the patriarchy, many women come so close to claiming that there is no such thing as menopause that they come very close to sounding like Mrs. Eddy.

I grew up hearing a very different sort of wishful thinking. My grandmother's disquisition on the menopause always began with a doleful sigh. "Ahhh! That time of life. . . . It's got to come to all of us someday."

In the South of my childhood, no woman could weather the "Change" completely unscathed; it was femininity's Appomattox and you had to milk it for every possible drop of theater.

A definite menopause class system existed. The Brahmins, of course, were the women who went hopelessly, gothically, permanently insane. In the next caste down were women with such severe female trouble that their "parts" fell out like gifts from a piñata, known as "she felt a *whoosh!* and then it just went *plop!*" The last of the Big Three patricians, officially disapproved of but providing a perfect plum of gossip, was the woman who developed another form of looseness known as "she *likes* men."

The pelvic bourgeoisie were the women who did "something peculiar," a catch-all phrase that might refer to a woman who became a spit-and-polish housekeeper after years of sloth; or one who took to shoplifting inane items like pen wipers; or one who suddenly began wearing white anklets (Granny: "whoopee socks") with black patent leather high heels.

The working class had the "sleeping Change," an extreme form of fatigue manifested by a neighbor of Granny's, who never did see the end of *The Sheik* despite ten trips to the theater. The phlegmatic quality of the sleeping Change made it déclassé because menopausal women are supposed to be "nervous." It always provoked the disappointed assessment, "She slept right through it," accompanied by a ski-slope gesture going off into infinity where, the speaker left no doubt, the calm one deserved to be banished.

The untouchables were the women who had no trouble whatsoever, known contemptuously as "She sailed right through it."

I started looking forward to the menopause at the age of twelve due to what male gynecologists call "discomfort"—wracking, knotting, waves of cramps and vomiting that lasted the whole of the first day and left me wrung out for most of the second. In high school I missed the annual French contest because of cramps. In college, as soon as the exam schedule was posted, I checked the dates in abject fear that one or more of mine would fall on Der Tag. Gradually my whole concept of time changed until I thought of a month as having twenty-five days of humanness and five others when I might just as well have been an animal in a steel trap. When I heard other women say, "My periods are what make me a woman," I always thought, "My periods are what keep me from being myself."

None of the doctors I consulted could find anything wrong with me. I thought I might have what Granny & Company called a "tilted womb" but my pelvis was normal in every way. Finally, at the age of thirty, I decided to try to get a partial hysterectomy. I picked that particular cut-off age because I had heard that a woman of thirty who had three children could have her tubes tied at her own request on the assumption that her whelping days were over (this was 1966). Since I did not intend to have any children at all, I figured that some version of the same rule would apply to me. (I was working for the *Raleigh News and Observer* and writing "30" at the end of copy, so it made a certain sense.)

One day while editing canned features I came across one about a contraceptive operation in which the lining of the uterus—the endometrium—is removed via the vagina. Without the porous lining, said the article, menstrual blood had no place to collect; the woman would stop menstruating, and her eggs, if fertilized, would simply slide down the slippery slope and be passed off unnoticed.

It sounded perfect. No surgery. Merely a matter of what Granny, in the fruitiness of her idiom, would have called: "They just reach right up and pull it right out—*whisk*!"

Feminists are right and wrong about male gynecologists. Yes, they are supercilious bastards; no, they are not swept by irresistible forces of sadism and greed at the thought of performing unnecessary operations on female organs—if they were, I would have gotten what I wanted.

The first one listened to my story, his mouth twitching in amusement, then patted my hand and said, "You'll change your mind when you hold your first baby in your arms."

The second one threw me out of his office.

"We have ways of curing monthly discomfort with medication! If you had a sore toe, would you want to get it cut off?"

"Sure, if it was sore enough," I said. "You can live with nine toes unless you're a ballet dancer, and I'm not."

"I hope you don't have children," he said, his voice shaking. "I'd hate to see what they'd turn out to be like."

A few weeks later while editing the social notes, I saw his daughter's name in a ballet recital list. Doubtless he was as sick of dying swans as I was of twat artists. I gave up the idea of having my endometrium ripped untimely from my womb and went on menstruating.

I began missing periods at forty-six and had my last one four years ago at fifty. Since then, I have been living proof of Simone de Beauvoir's assessment of menopause in *The Second Sex*:

> In many, a new endocrine balance becomes established. Woman is now delivered from the servitude imposed by her female nature, but she is not to be likened to a eunuch, for her vitality is unimpaired. And what is more, she is no longer the prey of overwhelming forces; she is herself, she and her body are one. It is sometimes said that women of a certain age constitute "a third sex"; and, in truth, while they are not males, they are no longer females. Often, indeed, this release from female physiology is expressed in a health, a balance, a vigor that they lacked before.

This is the calamity known as "losing your femininity" that women's magazines are so eager to help us stave off.

The prospect of being feminine always makes me think of James M. Cain's reply when asked to write for *The New Yorker*: "On the whole, I'd rather be dead."

In my youth I did a fairly credible imitation of femininity. I never could manage the big things, such as playing dumb or being undemanding in bed, but I did remember to soften my voice, shorten my stride, and be sweetly helpless about electricity. I played my part so well that eventually I came to believe it. It was easy to convince myself that I was feminine because I thought masculine women had to be athletic and good at sports, which I was not. It took the menopause to teach me that another, more agreeable kind of tomboyhood awaited me.

There are four stages of woman, best defined by looking at a commonplace task: taking the car to the shop. When you are a sweet young thing, the mechanics don't want you to hang around the shop for fear you will get dirty. When you are a sexy broad, they don't want you to hang around the shop for fear you will create such a tempting distraction that they will get hurt. And when you are a little old lady, they don't want you to hang around the shop for fear you will get in the way.

But there is another stage, the one between siren and dear old thing. Stage Three: sexually over the hill but still alert and able to move fast—*when the mechanics don't worry about you*! It lasts about fifteen years, from fifty to Social Security, but they are the best fifteen years of a woman's life; the debriefing years, the detoxification years, when she can shed her skin and become, for a brief shining moment, a female good ole boy.

It is de rigueur for post-menopausal women to say,

"I didn't get older, I got better," and describe how intense their orgasms are now that they no longer have to worry about getting pregnant.

There may be some women who suddenly discover that they "*like* men," but usually it's because they saved it up too long and must make up for lost time (Granny: "A candle always flares up before it goes out").

In the majority of cases, however, I suspect that the older-but-better brigade are fibbing in the cause of the American economy, which encourages them to do it. If the advertising-dependent women's magazines can make them believe that they never stop feeling horny, they will buy more clothes, cosmetics, vacations, plastic surgery, eighty-dollar haircuts, and Kellogg's Product 19 to feel like nineteen again even though it's as dry as a bone—and I don't mean the cereal.

The sacrilegious truth is, my sex drive diminished sharply when I started skipping periods, and vanished entirely as soon as they stopped for good. Now the only thing I miss about sex is the cigarette afterwards. Next to the first one in the morning, it's the best one of all. It tasted so good that even if I had been frigid I would have pretended otherwise just to be able to smoke it.

There is much to be said for post-menopausal celibacy. Sex is rough on loners because you have to have somebody else around, but now I don't. No more diets to stay slim and desirable: I've had sex and I've had food, and I'd rather eat. Although Mother Nature rather than willpower crafted my celibacy, the result has been the same. My powers of concentration are now as awesome as those of the most successful artistic or priestly practitioner of sublimation; sexual need no longer distracts me from my work.

There is a wholeness to celibacy. For a woman, a sexual relationship is an invasion of privacy, an absorption of individuality, a fragmentation of the personality

7

that poses an everpresent threat to the character. The
Roman historian Tacitus wrote: "When a woman has
lost her chastity she will shrink from no crime." He did
not mean that non-virgins routinely become murderers
and bank robbers, but that a woman in a sexual relationship makes emotional choices rather than ethical
ones—what Tammy Wynette was recommending when
she sang "Stand By Your Man." I never wanted to stand
by anybody except myself, and now I can.

Let's not forget the menopausal blessings of thrift.
My heating bill has gone down by more than half over
the last few years. So much, in fact, that a compassionate
soul from the utility company called me last winter to
see if I was in dire economic straits.

"If you've had financial difficulties we can enroll you
in our special payment plan," she said.

"I haven't had financial difficulties, I've had the
Change. My hot flashes keep me warm now. I've turned
into my own furnace."

"Oh. . . ."

I love those gulpy *oh's*. They are part and parcel of
another menopausal benefit I call the "boldness syndrome."

When I was menstruating, I used to avoid controversy because I was afraid that when the situation came
to a head, I wouldn't "feel well." Always, in the back of
my mind, lay the knowledge that if I shot off my mouth
on, say, the fourteenth of the month, that by the thir-
tieth, when everybody was good and mad, I would have
cramps and be unable to follow through. Now, I no
longer worry.

A woman must wait for her ovaries to die before she
can get her rightful personality back. Post-menstrual is
the same as pre-menstrual; I am once again what I was
before the age of twelve: a female human being who
knows that a month has thirty days, not twenty-five, and

who can spend every one of them free of the shackles of that defect of body and mind known as femininity.

The New-Old Me received the ultimate accolade a few months ago in Washington when I went up to the crime capital for a business meeting.

Walking back to my hotel alone in the early evening, I saw coming toward me two black boys of ten or twelve. Their body language was unmistakable; they were weaving like boxers and darting their heads to and fro, checking for police and adult males likely to come to my aid. It was obvious that they were getting ready to snatch my purse.

I tightened my grip on my shoulder strap. As we drew closer I saw their eyes moving over my face in quizzical examination. When we were almost abreast, one of them elbowed the other and waggled his head from side to side.

"Uh-uh. She a mean lady."

The mean lady grinned all the way back to the hotel, suffused in what bad novelists call a "sunburst feeling." The purse snatchers' decision to abort their mission was the most flattering compliment I have ever received from the male sex. They had acknowledged that I had lost my femininity, and it felt *great*.

I doubt if those two will ever read this book unless Marva Collins gets hold of them, but since there is no way to get in touch with them, I would like to leave them a message here.

"Bad-ass, the mean lady thanks you."

DO RIGHT:
THE THEORY

If Gary Hart does nothing newsworthy for the rest of his life, he will go down in history as the man who made a difference in American obsessions. For a few weeks during the 1988 campaign we stopped worrying about personality and started worrying about character.

In the South, the "character issue" comes under the heading of *Do Right*, as in: "You got to do right, you hear?"

The phrase defies precise one-sentence definitions, which is just the point. Wherever you find untranslatable culturisms you will also find the roots that rootless Americans crave. Moral certainties are the privilege of people who know who they are. The South is the only remaining American region with a strong identity. New England is gone as far as flinty Yankee virtues are concerned; people now say "the New England states" unless they're talking about autumn leaves. The midwest has turned into Middle America, which has turned into a demographic cliché, and the West has lost its former mystique and degenerated into a mere direction. But when Americans say *South*, they mean both states and a state of mind. It is this state of mind that produced Do Right.

Do Right is the South's Eleventh Commandment, a paradigmatic illustration of what the authors of *The Lonely Crowd* called "inner direction." A tangled credo that grew out of the old aristocratic ideal of honor, Do Right served the need for self-policing in isolated rural areas where your word really was your bond and having nothing except your good name was literally true. Do Right enabled Southerners to establish their bona fides at a time when computerized record-keeping was notably absent and men who sat on the porch with a rifle across their knees were notably present.

On the other side of the coin, because so much of Southern behavior was reprehensible if not illegal in Northern eyes, Do Right emerged as a compensatory mechanism, a kind of ethical dragnet to be cast in whatever direction the situation called for in the hope of scooping up as much honor as possible under the circumstances. Being *kind* to slaves, making *good* bootleg whiskey, and never shooting a man in the *back* all came under the heading of Do Right.

Do Right permits Southerners to combine conformity with rebellion and become notorious for both. Long before I ever heard of early Republican Rome's ideal of *virtus*, neoclassical France's ideal of the *honnête homme*, or John Ruskin's moral aesthetic, I was a walking computer loaded with Granny's Do Right software. I used it as a substitute for the Bible I was never made to read and the religion that my freewheeling Episcopalian family didn't practice to devise my own version of the Ten Commandments.

Captive of the voice in my head chanting, "*You got*

*to do right, you hear? . . . You got to do right, thass all. . . . I
mean, you got to do right, is all I'm sayin',"* I decided that
it was permissible to have an affair with a married man
provided 1.) I forbade him to criticize his wife in my
presence, 2.) I refused to let him spend any money on
me, and 3.) I quashed immediately and firmly any suggestion that he divorce his wife and marry me. Thus did
I write my own Golden Rule: fornicatrix, yes; Other
Woman, no. If that sounds quaint, it's precisely the kind
of quaintness America is hungering for when it agonizes
over preserving the traditional family.

By permitting us to practice situation ethics from an
unshakable moral base, Do Right endows Southerners
with a quality that we are never given credit for: sophistication. A case in point is Mississippi's notorious
"black market tax" on bootleg liquor. It has since been
repealed but the mindset that permitted it still flourishes
in sharp contrast to standard American naiveté. Our
blasé acceptance of the human comedy has something
in it of French ennui or European world-weariness that
recalls C. Vann Woodward's observation: "Southerners
are unburdened by the American delusion that nothing
is beyond our power."

Do Right takes many other forms. It's the trigger for
that touchy Southern pride that America's increasingly
passive citizenry would do well to study. Georgia writer
Rosemary Daniell provides a classic example of the Do
Right nervous system in her memoir, *Fatal Flowers*:

> Ted Hackett, an Atlanta psychotherapist who
> also practices in rural areas outside the city, ob-
> serves that Southerners tend to determine be-
> havior by a fixed set of ethics rather than by
> feeling or relationship. ("Why did you shoot your
> neighbor's dog?" "Because he peed on mah
> bushes." "You were angry because he peed on

your bushes?" "Nope, just shot 'em 'cause he peed on mah bushes.")

We do have a short fuse, but Do Right also endows us with a curious sense of fair play that can save others from us and us from ourselves. To me, the most shocking thing about the Howard Beach case, something that made it seem like an event in a remote foreign country, was that the white men chased the black man onto a busy freeway. Plenty of Southern men would not hesitate to beat up blacks, but that freeway sticks in my cultural craw. Transposing the scene to the South, I see *one* member of the white mob grabbing the black man by the collar at the last minute, pulling him back from the traffic and yelling, "You dumb nigger! You wanna git run over?" Translation: If you're mad enough, it's all right to kill somebody provided you do it fair and square, and provided you do it *yourself*. But don't chase him out into traffic and let someone else kill him for you, and then try to pass it off as an accident or involuntary manslaughter.

Do Right does heavy duty as tact. When William Faulkner embarked for Stockholm to receive the Nobel Prize, one of his neighbors said, "Now, Bill, you do right, you hear?" He meant, don't get drunk and fall on the King of Sweden.

Granny's shining example of Do Right as tact was played out at Colonial Beach, Virginia in 1941, when my tomboy mother rented a motorboat to take Granny, me, and our cousin Evelyn Cunningham for a ride.

"But Louise," Granny said dubiously. "Do you know how to drive a motorboat? Shouldn't we get one of the men?"

"Shit on the men, I can drive anything," Mama said with a swagger. "Come on."

As usual despite the heat, Granny wore a large straw

hat, a lace fichu, orange "service-weight" stockings, and as a concession to summer fun, white Enna Jettick laced oxfords instead of black ones. She made her stately way down to the dock and even managed to retain her dignity while Mama and Evelyn devised a system of human pulleys to get her into the boat. When she was settled at last in the bow, Mama started the motor.

"See?" she yelled triumphantly over the roar. "All you have to do is pull on that string!"

"Where did you learn this, Louise?" Granny shouted. "Who taught you?"

"Nobody! I saw it in the movies!"

We sliced through the muddy waves. At first it was dashing; Mama was wearing a blue yachting cap and making salty gestures, holding her palm up to her visor and peering knowledgeably off into the distance. She was in the middle of yelling "yo-ho-ho and a bottle of rum" when suddenly the motor died.

"Listen!" she said incongruously.

She yanked on the string but nothing happened. We were stuck in the middle of the Potomac.

"Louise!" Granny barked. "This is terrible!"

"Don't worry, Mother, Evelyn and I can row back. See, we've got emergency oars."

The oars were different sizes. After a few minutes of inexpert sideways rowing, Granny barked again.

"We're not going anywhere except around!"

"We'll get there eventually, Aunt Lura," Evelyn soothed. "We're not that far from shore. See? That's our cabin behind us."

It was behind us at the moment but ten minutes later it had vanished. Crablike, Mama and Evelyn were rowing toward the shore, but not the section of it that we wanted.

Some blistering time later while I was bailing out the

water they were splashing into the boat, Evelyn stopped rowing and raised her head.

"What's that singing?" she panted.

"Shall we gather at the river, where bright angel feet have trod. . . ."

We looked toward shore and saw something that made Granny emit a heartfelt cry of "Oh, no!" It was a group of white-robed black people standing in water up to their waists, conducting a total-immersion baptism on a deserted stretch of the segregated beach.

"We can't disrupt their service!" Granny cried. "Row away from them!"

"We're trying to, Mother!"

Just then a high-powered cabin cruiser appeared around the bend of the river and sped downstream. As it passed us, the waves from its wake joined forces with the panicky rowing to propel us straight into the arms of Jesus.

As we floated into the circle, the astonished worshippers parted ranks without missing a beat of the hymn. Mama and Evelyn pulled in their Mutt and Jeff oars and I shoved my bucket under the seat, but to mortified Granny there was only one way to Do Right.

"Sing!" she hissed.

We sang.

The lesson I imbibed that day was perhaps a bent one, but it was nonetheless character-forming. We had broken our end of the segregation bargain: if blacks had to stay off our turf, it followed that we had to stay off theirs. Years later during the sixties when an ostentatiously liberal Yankee took me to a black nightclub in Raleigh and spent the evening casting surreptitious eager glances at me to see if I was uncomfortable, he got the reaction he wanted. I *was* uncomfortable, but not for the reason he thought.

It is attitudes such as this that are trotted out as examples of Southern hypocrisy. Now that our little Yankee brothers have finally gotten it through their heads that hypocrisy is a synonym for civilization, the South has begun to look better and better to them. As the *Washington Times* noted in an editorial: "It is said, inevitably, that the Old South vote will be diluted by the Sunbelt immigrants who have moved down in the last ten or 15 years. But let us not forget that many of these Sunbelters moved down not just because of jobs but also because of deep-down stirrings toward Southernism."

One aspect of this increasingly appealing Southernism is the free-floating "niceness" that Yankees call "quality of life."

Wanna-be aristocrats work in mysterious ways, our wonders to perform. One of my earliest memories is of sitting at our oilcloth-covered dining table in whose center sat a can of Carnation milk with two holes punched in it, listening to Granny lecture on why "people like us" had to set a good example for the lower classes.

She called the Carnation milk "coffee cream." If the arching stream that spewed from the double opening happened to spill during the pouring, she wiped up the mess with a stained rag that she called a "tea towel." The crackpot noblesse oblige she promoted during our kaffeeklatches is the source of that very same free-floating niceness that free-farting America is presently seeking.

Like touchy pride and hair-trigger honor, Southern manners are an offshoot of the aristocratic spirit that we all like to think of as our birthright. Yankees constantly bite off "Have a good day" but it is rote and meaningless. By contrast, the psychic pressure points and trauma centers that operate on a we-never-close basis in the Do Right mind produce those grace notes of everyday Southern life that make all the difference.

Phrases such as "I've taken the liberty of . . . I'd be more than happy to . . . if you don't mind . . . if you would be good enough" are so redolent of a courtier's panache that a bad day can seem, in retrospect, to have been a good one.

Being raised by a Do Right grandmother who never spoke but spoke *ex cathedra* has had precisely the effect she intended: show me a value and I'll internalize it. It goes beyond continuing to ma'am and sir everything gray that moves despite my own fifty-four years (when I'm incarcerated in a nursing home I'll still have respect for age). My Do Rightism involves behavior that many feminists regard as female submissiveness, such as saying "Excuse me" when someone bumps into me, or "I'm sorry, you have the wrong number" even though it's I who have been inconvenienced.

It emerges in the kind of punctiliousness so scorned by laid-back permissive types, such as driving several miles out of my way to avoid backing up on a road marked *Private Property*. It also involves just plain compulsive behavior, such as my parallel parking number. The law says you must be no more than nine inches from the curb, so I go them one better and make my tires hug it. To make sure they are touching, I get out and run around to look. Every Southerner I've ever known does something of this sort, and the motivation for it is an internalized voice saying "Do right." When enough people twitch along in this manner, the result is a high quality of life.

There is, of course, a down side. Every ethical system contains the stumbling block of spiritual vanity. Religions produce mere hypocrites and pharisees, but Do Right produces monsters of egocentricity.

I always keep my word because I love being known as a person who always keeps my word. When I have a publishing deadline, being on time is not enough, I must be *early*. In social matters, pointless conventions are not merely the bee sting of etiquette but the snake bite of moral order, which revolves around *me*. Dreading the possibility that some *force majeure* will one day prevent me from keeping my word is my way of worrying about the environment. Never mind nuclear weapons, oil spills, and the ozone layer, there is only one threat to life as we know it: if I break a promise, the entire universe will turn into a necrotic pit.

Purveyors of caring 'n' compassion who preach putting others above self might do well to reflect that the egocentricity of Do Right is what makes the honor system work.

Take, for example, the day the bookcase fell on me as I was rearranging the apartment to accommodate my new photocopier. Naturally I was smoking while I worked. As long as I stayed in the dining room I could put the cigarette down in the ashtray on the table, but when I had to stretch a wire into the spare bedroom, I hit an ethical fork in the road. Halfway there with a cigarette dangling from my mouth, the little silver bell of Do Right tinkled in my head. *Walkin' with a cigarette in your mouth looks downright trashy!* so I took it out and started back to the dining room to put it in the ashtray.

I never got there. I'm not really sure how it happened, only that there were all these wires all over the place, and several pieces of furniture I had moved were in unfamiliar locations. The point is, *I was alone in the apartment*. Nobody could see me with the cigarette in my mouth, but *I* could see me, which meant that the whole world could see me.

Do Right is such a powerful force in the South that the phrase is also used as an idiom to describe inanimate objects that break or don't work. When my new vacuum cleaner went on the blink after only two weeks, I took it back to the store and said to the woman behind the complaint desk, "This dudden do right."

She knew exactly what I meant. We had a dishonorable vacuum cleaner on our hands.

DO RIGHT:
THE PRACTICE

In 1961 I was living in a studio apartment in Washington, writing true confessions and going out on Manpower temp jobs whenever the belles-lettres kitty got too low.

I was in no position to meet the kind of people who gave status parties, but my father was. It was a year when every college kid in America wanted to be a folk singer, so Herb was giving banjo and guitar lessons to the whelps of the Establishment. Among his pupils was the son of a member of the White House press corps. One day, Herb and I happened to run into the boy's mother downtown and she invited us to have a drink with her in the Mayflower Hotel. In this roundabout fashion I got invited to a real, honest-to-God "Washington party" at which I was the only native Washingtonian.

There I met a woman whom I shall call Reba.

Technically there is no such thing as a quack literary

agent because agents have no licensing or educational requirements. Those who can, do; those who can't, don't. Thanks to this casual arrangement, a lot of writers have an agent story but I defy anyone to top mine.

Reba was in her late forties and fighting it. When she found out I had published all those true confessions, her eyes stretched open as wide as her temple tucks permitted.

"How would you like to edit the memoirs of Sophie von Nagelspeer?"

I looked blank and she rushed on.

"She's had the most *fascinating* life. Been everywhere, done everything, a real citizen of the world. Name a war or a revolution and Sophie's been through it. *And* you'll never guess whose mistress she was!"

She named a Balkan war lord I had never heard of: Count Stanislaus Lidic.

"She's load—er, she's very well off," Reba amended carefully. "She'll pay you a hundred dollars just to read the manuscript. If you decide you want to work on it, she'll pay three hundred a month, and I *know* I can get you a percentage of the book's earnings. You can do it at home in your spare time."

That last had the ring of matchbook covers and back-of-the-book pulp magazine ads. Its echo hung between us, giving Reba a rich air of fraudulence that intrigued me the way snakes intrigue birds, or mongooses intrigue snakes, or whatever that fateful stand-off is.

As con artists always do in such moments, Reba whipped out that American version of a Potemkin village, an engraved business card, and thrust it into my hand.

"Think about it and call me," she said, and hurried off.

It was a big party and I did not see her again that night, but my thoughts kept returning to her and her

21

roving margravin. Writer's curiosity is a terrible thing; we get ourselves into the most ungodly messes and then rationalize whatever happens with "I was only gathering experience." Sensing that there was something about Reba that did not add up, I could not resist the chance to study her *and* meet the last of the Hapsburg doxies as well. The next day I fished out her card and called her, and she invited me for cocktails with Sophie von Nagelspeer.

Like many bona fide literary agents, Reba worked out of her apartment. It was a solid old building in a good neighborhood that catered to the fairly prosperous, and sported a South American doorman. When I told him whose guest I was, his eyes shifted momentarily; clearly there was something about my new acquaintance that disturbed him. My curiosity mounted.

I took the elevator up to Reba's floor and rang her bell. The door was opened by a girl in her late teens whose sweetly bland face made me think of anachronistic expressions like "placid shepherdess" and poems like "Come Into the Garden, Maud." She wore a schoolgirl uniform of dark green jumper and plain white shirtwaist that looked institutional but expensive. It was like coming face-to-face with one of Miss Brodie's girls.

"Hi! You must be Mummy's friend, Florence. I'm Poppy."

Reba stuck her head around the kitchen door and waved me into the living room. The apartment was luxuriously furnished, with real crystal cocktail equipment. I sat down on the long beige sofa and Poppy took a straight chair, folding her hands and sitting as primly as a classroom monitor. She was, as Granny would have said, "just as sweet as she could be."

Too sweet, I decided. Something was wrong here.

Reba emerged from the kitchen. "Sophie will be a little late. Would you like a martini?"

She mixed the cocktails, then sat down opposite me and said, "Well!"

We had an innocuous getting-to-know-you conversation. As we talked she kept glancing nervously at my hair in its chignon on top of my head. Chignon being a fancy word for *bun*, it was guaranteed to upset determinedly glamorous women like Reba—one reason I wore it that way. She was much too smooth to come out with that lower-middle-class thrust, "I'd *love* to get my hands on your hair," but I could tell she was thinking it.

She patted her bleached blond beehive with calculated absent-mindedness and trailed her fingers down her temple tucks. In an ever-so-ladylike way, she scratched them. I wondered suddenly if such women were given to petty cruelty because they itched all the time. Between the biting peroxide, the rigidly glued hair spray, the wired bra, the pinching girdle, and the plastic surgery, she must have been on fire. I made a mental note—*"cattiness as relief"*—and hoped I would remember to transfer it to my journal when I got home.

"I must see to those hors d'oeuvres," she murmured, rising. As she crossed in front of me on her way to the kitchen, she sucked in her gut West Point-style and ran her palms over the knobs of her pelvis bones. While she was rummaging in the fridge the doorbell rang.

"I'll get it, Mummy," Poppy called solicitously. Then, turning to me, "Would you excuse me, please?"

She scampered into the foyer. I heard her open the door and say *"gnädige Frau."* The guest replied in a glottal rumble that was drowned out by the bustling sounds of arrival. There was a rattle of paper bags, followed by a rattle of coat hangers, but the guest said, "I keep mein coat" and strode into the living room.

I stood up.

Sophie von Nagelspeer was a statuesque five-feet-ten

or so even with her dowager's hump, and bore herself with an air of faded magnificence that extended from the top of her white head to the soles of her Red Cross oxfords. It was easy to see that she had been, as Southerners put it, "a raving beauty in her day." Her square face was crisscrossed with so many wrinkles that she looked like a Teutonic forest queen who had been caught in acid rain, but the cheekbones under the ravaged skin were so high that her eyes slanted like the blades of an opened pair of scissors.

The coat she had insisted on keeping was real mink, but judging from its New Look hemline grazing her ankles, she must have acquired it around 1947. Her big hands were loaded with dirty diamonds; in one she carried a pocketbook the size of a small suitcase and in the other a bulging Woodward & Lothrop shopping bag containing the manuscript of her memoirs.

Reba introduced us but she really didn't have to. It was, to mix an ethnic metaphor, a case of Greek meets Greek. Sophie reminded me of Granny and all the other bustling, imperious dowagers I had ever known. For her part, it was obvious that I had won her authoritarian heart by leaping to my feet and giving her my best South Prussian "ma'am."

Swathed in the voluminous coat, she sat down and accepted a martini. After taking a disinterested ritual sip, she pointed a thick finger at me.

"She ist old zoll."

"An old soul," Reba repeated, looking from Sophie to me with a nervous smile. "Isn't that fascinating? Sophie believes in reincarnation, you know."

"I think there's something to it," I said.

"I don't zink it, I *know* it. Reincarnation ist a fact, zere ist no argument. Ve haf met bevorr, Florenz, in anudder life. Zer moment I zaw you, I know ve haf good karma."

24

Reba's head swiveled harder, her expression taking on a revealing contradictory mixture of relief and consternation. On the one hand, she was glad that the two people she intended to use had hit it off so well; on the other hand, she was worried that too strong an alliance between the marks might work against her. Hurriedly, she changed the subject.

"*I* feel like the oldest soul in town with this weather we've been having. So drying! I've used *tons* of moisturizer but it doesn't help. Do you know what does? A masque! I've discovered a marvelous new kind. I wear it in the tub and it just *melts* the wrinkles away!"

"You vear a mask in zer bazztub?" Sophie asked with alarm. "Mein lover, Count Lidic, vas azzazzinated in zer bazztub because he vas vearing his gazz mask und could not zee vrom zer steam to defend himzelf. Ist in zer book," she added, patting the shopping bag.

A silence fell. I tried futilely to place the event in history. Reba looked bewildered.

"Mummy doesn't mean that kind of mask, *gnädige Frau*," Poppy said politely. "She means a cosmetic mask, like a mud pack."

"It contains avocado, you just *slather* it on and let it set."

"Oh," grunted Sophie, obviously bored.

"Why was Count Lidic wearing a gas mask in the bathtub?" I asked.

"Because his spies told him zat his enemies planned to zrow cyanide pellets in zer vindow, zo he alvays vore a gazz mask ven he bazed," Sophie explained. "But instead zey burst in zer door und garroted him." She twisted an imaginary rope in her hands. "I like to zink he died as he vanted. He alvays said zat a true revolutionary does not die on zer barricades, but in zer bazztub—he vas a great admirer of Marat."

Reba was now completely lost, and I was still combing

through my useless college education to locate Count
Lidic in *Problems in European Realignment: 1815–1914.*

"Where did this happen?" I asked.

"Budapest, vere else?" Sophie said with a shrug.

"Spoken like a true Viennese," Reba caroled. "Well,
now, shall we get down to business?"

Before she could get any further, Sophie handed me
the bulging shopping bag and opened her huge purse.
To my surprise and Reba's bug-eyed astonishment, she
pulled out a hundred-dollar bill and stuck it in my jacket
pocket, giving my hip a little pat.

"I know you are honest, zo I pay in advanz."

"You shouldn't carry so much cash around, Sophie,"
Reba warned. Her voice dropped to a stage whisper.
"All this crime nowadays."

Sophie gave a cavalier wave. "I haf known real danger."

When I got home, I made a big pot of coffee and
prepared to stay up all night reading Sophie's memoirs.
The shopping bag contained four typing-paper boxes.
I opened the one marked *Vol. I* and looked at the title
page.

SWIFTING TO EAGLE TRILL

I was sure she had meant "Swiftly Flies the Eagle,"
or "Swiftly, As the Eagle." What stumped me was the
trill. Did eagles trill?

When I turned to the epigraph page I saw that the
title had come from a poem she had written.

> Swifting to eagle trill
> Footing bat for time, Wilhelm,
> Is short in boslings.
> Into the gims of time of time
> When all is pall and hallwood

> To an unstoned turn
> Of virtuous rubies.

When I had struggled through the first chapter I was able to decode most of the poem. Sophie was the daughter of an Austrian count. At fourteen she had fallen in love with a footman named Wilhelm who had been her father's batboy, or orderly, when Count von Nagelspeer had served in the Imperial Army. Finding his daughter and his servant in a compromising situation in the stable, the count shot Wilhelm and shipped Sophie off to a convent.

Pall and *hallwood* were the Biblical warnings about gall and wormwood from the Book of Revelations, and *virtuous rubies* was a variation on the famous scriptural puff about the virtuous woman, "her price is above rubies." I had no idea what *bosling* and *gims* were, but *unstoned turn* was obviously her version of "leave no stone unturned," a reference to her successful effort in escaping the convent.

The poem wasn't all that needed decoding. The whole book was written the same way—all four boxes of it. Sophie had some sort of problem with words. Her spoken English, though heavily accented, made sense, but when she put pen to paper her brain scrambled words and invented new ones. Her style would have made a postcard difficult, but she had written three thousand pages about Serbian noblemen disguised as Montenegrin goatherds, and Montenegrin goatherds disguised as Serbian noblemen. There was no way to edit or revise it. It needed to be drastically cut and completely rewritten, and whoever did it stood an excellent chance of ending up in the funny farm.

Judging from the tattered condition of the manuscript, it had made the rounds of every agent and publisher in *The Literary Market Place* and *The Writer's Market*,

until it and its author had fallen into the clutches of
Reba, who was in neither.

Thinking of the hundred-dollar bill Sophie had
given me, I wondered how someone with her checkered
past could be so trusting. Some hours later, after strug-
gling through a few more chapters of her memoirs, I
began to understand. This woman had waltzed with men
whose faces bore Heidelberg dueling scars. Honor in all
its passé forms—Old World, belle époque, Junker,
Hapsburg, noblesse oblige—was the foundation of her
character.

She had never done anything really wrong; her sins
had been confined to what Mrs. Patrick Campbell called
"the hurly-burly of the chaise longue." Despite jewelry
smuggling, forged papers, and her part in all the plots
and counterplots of Middle European politics, she had
rigid standards of behavior and she had never lost the
innocent conviction that other people shared them.

It was a mindset that an unreconstructed Southerner
understood and an alienated American appreciated.
Sophie and Reba were made to order for my Alpha-
and-Omega temperament; the situation had all the ingredients of a Do Right passion play and I couldn't resist
it. I decided to get involved.

I spent the weekend reading Sophie's book. Reba
called twice to ask me if I thought it was good, thereby
proving that she hadn't read it. She kept trying to in-
troduce the subject of a contract binding Sophie and me
to her "agency," but I put her off, saying that I needed
to do more thinking about creative matters before we
got into nuts and bolts.

I suspected that she intended to draw me into a plan
to help her milk Sophie dry, and then turn around and
screw me out of my share. Sophie being such an obscure
adventuress, there was very little chance of the book
being taken by a legitimate house no matter how well it

was written, so Reba probably had a crony lined up to pose as a vanity press publisher. The two of them would extort exorbitant publishing costs from Sophie and divvy it up between them, leaving her and me holding the bag.

Even though Sophie had held on to her ill-gotten gains and had money to burn, I didn't want to see her get cheated. I was unequipped to beat Reba at her own game, so there was no point in trying to diddle her in matters like the wording of contracts. The thing to do was see to it that Sophie and I did not sign anything at all.

As for the book, once I got her pried away from Reba, I could put the manuscript into good enough shape and reasonable length so that if she wanted to take it to a legitimate vanity publisher later on, she could do so.

The following Friday Reba invited us both over for another cocktail-hour meeting. I arrived a little after the appointed time but the door was opened by Reba wearing nothing but a small towel.

"Hi! I'm running late and Poppy's off with some of her little friends. I just got out of the tub. Come in the bedroom and talk to me while I dress. Sophie won't be along for a while yet."

I followed her into the bedroom and sat down on one end of a pink velvet love seat shaped like a coiled serpent. I was no sooner settled than Reba tossed her towel aside and began doing stretching exercises in the nude.

"It . . . tones . . . the . . . muscles," she panted.

Standing directly in front of me, she stuck one leg straight up in the air and grabbed hold of the ankle like a can-can dancer. I had a choice of looking at her, or making an awkward point of not looking at her, so I looked. She had bleached her pubic hair, not just the stomach puff but all of it—chalk up another itch. She was exposing herself in a trancelike way, as if she were so accustomed to using sex to achieve her aims that she did it automatically, whether it was necessary or not, whenever she was confronted by someone whose co-operation she needed: a busy plumber, a Hertz girl with one car left, or me. She had confidence, did our Reba. She also had piles and, I believe, a cervical polyp.

"What . . . do . . . you . . . think . . . of . . . Sophie's . . . book?"

"It needs to be completely rewritten."

She dropped her leg and smiled wolfishly. "That bad, eh? Well, that calls for a bigger piece of the action than we thought, doesn't it? Say, a ghosting fee of ten thousand payable in three installments and split sixty-forty between you and the agency?"

"There'd be a lot of work involved," I said noncommittally.

"And, um, a marketing fee, since Sophie is an unpublished author?"

"Marketing an unknown is always hard."

She appraised me with a smirky, overconfident look that made me mad. Writers always resent the stereotype that people like Reba have of us. They think we're naive, impractical, ivory-tower intellectuals who can be hoodwinked in business matters. While this is largely true, it has a flip side: Hell hath no fury like a liberal arts major scorned.

Reba got dressed. She had just finished putting on her face when the doorbell rang.

It was Sophie. This time she embraced me and called me her *kleine* something. We had martinis and Reba stated her terms.

"Ja, ja, ja," Sophie agreed impatiently. "Ten zousand vor zer writing ist fine. Meet me in vront of my bank tomorrow at noon und I vill vizzdraw zer money und pay you."

That's when Reba blew it. Thinking *contract*, and doubtless savoring all the low blows she was planning to deliver in fine print, she was so taken aback by Sophie's instant compliance and her abrupt offer to pay the whole advance up front that she turned down the chance for a simple, old-fashioned, cash-on-the-barrel sting in favor of a modern, convoluted paper chase that would make her feel like a real literary agent. The American worship of credentials had done her in.

"Ooooh, noooo! We have to put it *in writing*."

As soon as she said it she looked as if she wanted to fall on her nail file. Realizing her mistake, her eyes stretched open so wide that she nearly split her temple tucks. She looked like a silent film villain getting ready to say, "Zzzzzt! Foiled again!"

She had given me the perfect cue to do what I wanted to do.

"I don't think we need to put anything in writing," I said, "and I don't think we should go to the bank either. Sophie, you trusted me last time when you handed over your manuscript and a hundred dollars, now I'm going to return the compliment. I'll rewrite your book on good faith alone. We don't need a contract. A handshake is enough."

As her big hand crushed mine, I felt as though I had reached out and touched a vanished world, one in which a gentleman always paid his gambling debts, and the most depraved roués confined their seductions to married women because they would never dream of "compromising" a virgin.

Reba was nonplused. There was nothing she could say except "How do you expect me to cheat you without a contract?" Since she couldn't very well say it, she mixed another round of martinis and sat quietly sipping hers while Sophie spent the rest of the cocktail hour talking about reincarnation. She perked up a little towards the end, indicating that the wheels were turning anew, but I decided to worry about her later. For the moment I had achieved my goal.

Do Right can really be the pits. Having promised to rewrite the book on spec, I now had to do so. In desperation I contemplated turning it into an historical novel, another *Prisoner of Zenda* with lots of sex, but costume romance wasn't selling in the relevancy-crazed sixties. In any case, Sophie's background of pre-World War I Balkan politics was much too complicated to dramatize. Now I could appreciate Queen Mary's outburst at the height of the Abdication crisis: "Really, this might be Rumania!" Every faction had a femme fatale, every leader was named Anton or Stepan, and people kept throwing each other out of windows. I settled for heavy cutting and sane English and went on with my decoding.

Shortly after I started on the third box, Reba decided to give a party. A firm believer in getting work out of people for free, she asked me if I would come over that Saturday morning and help her get things ready.

When I rang the bell, the door was opened by Poppy the placid shepherdess.

"Hi! You're *so* good to come and help us," she effused in her gracious little lady way.

The kid intrigued me as much as Reba. In a year when everyone else her age looked like a flea-bitten mendicant, she didn't even wear jeans for housework. This morning she had on a blouse and a little pair of pastel pedal pushers with an old bath towel pinned around her waist.

As we polished the silver, she chatted gaily about school in a high-pitched, innocent voice, interspersing her remarks with "Mummy says." It was so quaint, so genteel, so contentedly English, that I could not connect it to Reba's rootless stalk through life. By the time I left to go home to dress I was so thoroughly puzzled that I gave up trying to figure it out and took refuge in a Southern explanation: Poppy must have inherited enough "good blood" from her father's side to offset her mother's "bad blood."

She walked me to the door like a class guide on Founders Day; I could almost see a blue bandolier affixed with a politeness medal draped across her shoulder.

"I hope you like my soup," she said. "I'm making a huge pot of cream of shrimp. Poor Mummy's been working so hard, I told her I'd do it."

That evening I picked Sophie up in a cab and we went over to Reba's together. The first person we saw was the South American doorman pacing the lobby and clutching his face. Recognizing us, he flailed his arms and loosed a torrent of hysterical Spanish interspersed with sobs.

"Vot ist?" Sophie demanded.

He pointed to the ceiling. "Your friend ... she scream ... trap een bathtub ... much water."

We hurried to the elevator. During the maddeningly slow assent to Reba's floor, the doorman sobbed out the rest of the story.

"The daughter, she have knife. She say she keel me when I go een apartment. She tie the mama een the tub for to drowning her."

"Did you call the police?" I asked.

"No, ees too dangerous."

When he opened Reba's door with his pass key, we heard a furious rush of water and a bellow of rage from Mummy Dearest.

"LET ME OUT OF HERE, YOU FUCKING LIT-TLE CUNT!"

"OLD WHORE!" Poppy screamed back. "YOUR CUNT'S AS BIG AS A BUCKET! OCCUPATIONAL HAZARD—HA! HA! HA!"

Water was seeping from under the bathroom door and logging the foyer carpet. As Sophie and I squished in, Poppy ran out of the bedroom waving a butcher knife. When she saw Sophie, she ground to a halt and dropped a curtsy.

"Welcome, *gnädige Frau*. Thank you *so* much for telling the story about Count Lidic. It inspired me to murder Mummy in the bathtub."

"YOU LITTLE BITCH! I'LL PUT YOU IN A REAL REFORM SCHOOL THIS TIME, NOT THAT SICKIE ACADEMY! OPEN THIS FUCKING DOOR!"

Sophie threw her well-upholstered self against the door until it flew open. A hellish cloud of steam billowed out and enclosed us in a wet, gauzy embrace. As we stumbled in, Poppy hung back emitting maniacal cackles.

Sophie opened the window and I turned off the rushing faucets. When the steam cleared we saw Reba seated in the overflowing tub holding an enormous soup tureen. Knotted around her neck was a rope whose other end was tied to the shower nozzle. Her avocado masque had turned into a sepulchral deposit of slimy lumps that dripped off her face and spattered on her bosom like coagulated green blood.

I took the soup tureen. Reba rose up and lunged for Poppy, causing the noose to tighten and drag her back into the tub with a horrendous splash. As Sophie struggled to untie the rope, I noticed a very bad smell coming from the tureen. Lifting the lid, I saw that Poppy had used it for a chamber pot. No wonder Reba had to hold on to it after Poppy handed it to her; she could not let go of it unless she wanted to swim in its contents, and she could not lean over the edge of the tub and put it on the floor without hanging herself. Count Lidic's demise might have been the conscious inspiration for Poppy's deed but on an unconscious level it was a bow to the four corners of the temple of motherhood: feeding, bathing, toilet training, and umbilical cords.

Sophie got the noose undone and Reba leaped out of the tub. Her dry skin was now so soft and puckered that it looked as if it were about to fall off.

"I'LL SUE THAT FUCKING SCHOOL FOR LET-TING YOU OUT! I'LL SUE THAT FUCKING SHRINK! I'LL SLIT YOUR GODDAMN THROAT!"

Poppy gave chase and they tore through the apartment throwing things at each other. When they got to the buffet table they started throwing food. Just then some more party guests arrived and walked through the open door. One of them was another of Reba's "clients," a prizefighter-turned-writer who never said anything except "fuck Proust." Even that deserted him now as he watched the food fight in open-mouthed wonder, completely inarticulate at last.

Seeing the crowd clustered in the doorway, the avocado-speckled Reba shrieked and ran naked past them into her bedroom like a green sprite fresh from an old grave.

"People!" Poppy called out. "Come in and I'll tell you a story. I just got out of a school for crazy kids where Mummy had to send me after I escaped from the Texas oil man she sold me to, the one who liked to stick candy canes up my ass. Mummy's been blackmailing him and living on the money!"

Before anyone could comment, she opened the window and leaned out to yell at the people on the street.

"THIS IS REBA'S WHORE HOUSE! WE NEVER CLOSE! WE FUCK AND SUCK AND BLO-O-O-W-W THE HOUSE DOWN! ASS FOR SALE! ASS FOR SALE!"

Sophie gripped my arm with her big fingers. "Come. Ve leaf."

When we got down to the lobby the police were coming in the front door, but we made such a respectable-looking pair that they didn't even glance at us.

She took me to her favorite *landsmann* restaurant and treated me to a spread of stuffed pork roast, hot potato salad, red cabbage, and beer. Any other woman would have immediately launched a gossipy postmortem of the scene we had just witnessed, but she made no mention of Reba during the entire meal, so I took the hint and said nothing about her either.

Nor did she mention her book. In a graceful manner she drew me out and got me to talk about myself. I told her about my family, my schooling, my hopes, and she listened raptly in a way that was immensely flattering. It occurred to me that this was the way she must have listened to all those hussars and cuirassiers who found her so fascinating. No wonder men were so susceptible to such blandishments. . . . I was susceptible to them myself.

When the coffee came I fell silent and Sophie asked me no more prompting questions. After a moment she reached across the table and patted my hand and gave me a wistful smile.

"I haf made new plans. I vas going to tell you und Reba tonight. I go back to Vienna next veek . . . vor good. You zee, I go to zer doctor und he tell me I haf not long to lif." She tapped her heart. "I haf been a vanderer vor zo long, but now, after zer doctor tell me, I decide I do not vant to die in—you vill pardon me— a foreign country. I vant to go home."

She looked beyond me into the past, swaying her heavy shoulders under the ratty mink as if waltzing to her memories. After a moment she came out of her reverie and reached into her gigantic pocketbook.

"You vork on zer book vor tree months. Zat ist nine hundred dollars. Here ist."

She handed me nine hundred-dollar bills, the original figure Reba had quoted me on the night we met, before she began brainstorming.

"Don't you want me to finish it?"

"Nein, nein, ist over."

She laid some more bills on the check, gave the waiter a keep-the-change wave, and hauled herself out of the booth with a flourish of still-damp mink. Out on the street, she used another grand gesture to hail a cab. It stopped on a dime.

"I drop you."

She said nothing on the way to my apartment. I wanted to ask her if she wanted her manuscript back. I wanted to ask her if she had any friends or relatives left in Vienna, I wanted to suggest that we write to each other, but everything I wanted to say would have been a clumsy anticlimax. Her "ist over" had said it all. She was a master of the civilized social art that eludes Americans: she knew how to be a ship that passed in the night.

When the cab pulled up at my door I said the only thing left to say.

"Goodbye."

"Nein," she smiled, touching my cheek. "Till ve meet again."

I kept her manuscript for years, finally burning it after the publication of several books of my own had made it possible for me to buy a condo with a fireplace. While the flames consumed the yellowed pages I put Strauss waltzes on the stereo and toasted her memory with champagne.

It seemed like the right thing to do.

EVERYBODY'S
GOTTA RIGHT
TO BE FAMOUS

When I toured my first book in 1975 I appeared as the
mystery guest on the national game show "To Tell the
Truth." Some weeks later on the day after the show
aired, I was walking to the grocery store when suddenly
I heard a screech of wheels. Certain that I was about to
be run over, I jumped into somebody's yard and shrank
behind a concrete flower pot.

A station wagon had braked to a stop. In it were a
man, a woman, and three children. They spoke in un-
ison.

"We saw you on television!"

It was the first time I ever saw what I now think of
as "The Look." A smiling frown; pleased yet offended,
knowing yet puzzled, contented yet demanding, placid
yet aroused, ready to kiss and ready to kill. A whole
thesaurus of conflicting emotions in one Chevy telling

me that I had done something right that was wrong, and something wrong that was right.

I had looked into the ultimate conundrum of American equality: the adoring hatred that the obscure feel for the famous.

Thanks to an accident of birth, I have an attitude toward famous people that is rare in America. As a native of Washington, D.C., I grew up seeing presidents and other leaders frequently, the way natives of Los Angeles grow up seeing movie stars. Granny and I saw Eleanor Roosevelt busily going through the rack of $3.95 dresses in the basement of the Woodward & Lothrop department store, and Mama and I ran into Bess Truman in the Fannie May candy store at 17th and Pennsylvania Avenue across from the White House. We saw Teddy Roosevelt's daughter and Woodrow Wilson's widow several times, as well as numerous congressmen who, in those simpler times, were in the habit of riding the streetcar.

My first exposure to celebrity as we know it today occurred when I was six or seven and Frank Sinatra was singing on the radio. Walter Winchell aired regular reports about the behavior of Sinatra's screaming fans. They pulled buttons off his coat, grabbed his gloves off his hands, and invaded restaurants to salvage scraps from his plate. As his fame grew, the gossip columns filled up with stories of his reaction to it all. He started slugging people, which landed him squarely on Granny's fighting side.

"That boy wasn't properly reared," she decreed. "When people admire and look up to you, it's your *duty* to be gracious and kind."

Properly implanted gyroscopes continue to beep long after the planter has been planted. When I began getting fan mail, I heard Granny's voice in my head: "*If people are good enough to write to you. . . .*"

I answered every letter, and I answered them promptly—so promptly that I was embarrassed whenever my publishers dragged their feet, as publishers will, about forwarding my mail. Afraid that someone would think that *I* had waited a month to answer, I made a point of explaining that I had just received the letter from New York.

Answering my mail was far from a grim duty, however, because I consider my readers sacred. To my added delight I found most of them to be intelligent and interesting. If they asked specific questions I answered them in as much detail as possible; if they simply said, "I loved your book," I sent a postcard saying, "Thank you so much for writing."

Several especially pleasant fan mail encounters stick in my mind:

When a certain national newsmagazine paraphrased me to the point of plagiarism, a reader whom I had heard from before wrote me again to say that I should sue them, and offered to sign a deposition for me.

A woman who read one of my *Cosmopolitan* articles picked up on a passing reference I made about the fourteenth-century romance between John of Gaunt and Lady Katherine Swynford. She had loved Anya Seton's novel, *Katherine*, and wanted to know if I had read it too. I had—that's where I got the reference. A day or so later while browsing in a second-hand book store I came across a print of a medieval woman. I bought it and sent it to my correspondent, saying, "This looks just like our Katherine." She wrote back to thank me and we exchanged a few extremely enjoyable letters before losing touch.

The day after the publication of *Confessions of a Failed Southern Lady*, a young man who runs a rare book store called me immediately after finishing it. Because he was the first fan of a new book, I sent him an autographed copy. He responded with a beautiful edition of *The Letters of Henry Adams* with gilt-edged pages—the only really nice book I've ever had. We have been corresponding ever since, and I have a standing invitation to dinner whenever I'm in his city.

Experiences like these are one reason why I listed myself under my full name and address in the phone book. The other reason has to do with my version of democracy: ego, yes; conceit, no. Or: elitism, yes; status symbols, no. The unlisted number has gone the way of BMWs, Nike running shoes, and thirty-dollar jars of mustard and I want no part of any of them.

It was too good to last. My excellent track record ended last year with a nightmarish incident that says a little about me and a lot about America.

I got the following letter from two women:

> Dear Florence:
> We are writing this letter to you (assuming you are the famous authoress Florence King), to thank you for *Confessions of a Failed Southern Lady* and to confess that while we were on vacation we brazenly stole: 1.) *When Sisterhood Was in Flower*, 2.) *Southern Ladies and Gentlemen*, 3.) *Wasp, Where Is Thy Sting?* and 4.) first edition *Confessions* from a public library. We stole these books because after reading *Confessions* we both became Florence King fanatics, and being unable to locate these treasures from any bookstores in our town, were led to our current life of common library crime! (Note: *He: An Irreverent Look At the Amer-*

ican Male is missing from all the sources we have checked . . . got any ideas??)

Now Florence, it's only right that these stolen books go back to where they belong, but we re-fuse to return them unless you send us two signed copies of *Confessions*. If you meet our de-mands, we promise to return all of the stolen Florence King masterpieces to the libraries from which they came. (Our check for fifty hard-earned dollars is enclosed with a million thanks and the promise to be the two founding members of the Florence King Fan Club.)

With love and thanks we remain. . . .

Enclosed were photos of themselves holding the stolen library copies of my books.

I was a little put off by the first-naming, but what snagged my eye was the subtle note of threat in the line, "*If you meet our demands. . . .*" I procrastinated for two weeks, uncertain whether to answer them. If I did not, it would be the first fan letter I ever ignored, and that bothered me as much as the threat line. I changed my mind several times before I finally decided to go ahead and do it, telling myself that the terrorist phrasing was simply a manifestation of something I had run into many times: when you're billed as a humorist, people feel chal-lenged to try to make you laugh.

I also told myself—this is so Protestant—that the check they had enclosed was proof of their bona fides. It was more than enough to cover the cost of the books—much more than enough in view of my forty-percent author's discount. I decided that they had paid more than necessary to avoid the embarrassment of pay-ing less—just the sort of thing I would do. This inter-pretation made me feel so relieved that I even debated sending them my check for the overpayment, but there's a line between Do Right and Miss Goody Two-Shoes so I let it go.

I signed two copies of *Confessions* in the standard fashion—"Especially for. . . . with all best wishes"—and mailed them off.

I thought that would be the end of it, but a week or so later I got two effusive thank-you notes. One of them concluded: *"You may rightly read between the lines here and know that I would give anything to meet you. (I also travel a lot and would be in Fredericksburg in a second!)"*

Oh, Jesus. . . .

I ignored both notes. A month or more passed with no more word from them. I relaxed, figuring that it was really over now, but then I got a letter they had written together.

> Dear Florence:
>
> We have read *Confessions* so many times and love it so much, we now yearn to have a picture of the people you brought to life in the book. Would you *by any chance* have a picture that might include Herb, Louise, Granny, yourself, and possibly Jensy? We wouldn't dream of taking an original from you, but if you have a spare picture or one we could make a copy of, we would be thrilled. It would be truly wonderful to see the faces of these dear people. If this request causes the needle of your nuisance meter to go off the scale, please feel free to blatantly shun your most devoted fans!
>
> Our gratitude endures. Love. . . .

The sadomasochistic dare in that last sly sentence made me mad. I knew I should ignore the letter but nobody was going to play head games with me. I wanted to have the last word and I wanted it to be a very curt last word. My father, like most Englishmen, could commit assault and battery with politeness, so I decided to use his technique.

I wrote back, addressing them formally as "Dear Miss _____ and Miss _____" and said: "My only family pictures are pasted in an album or framed and hung on the wall. Since you have expressed enjoyment of my writing, I suggest that a more interesting and constructive way to follow my fortunes is to subscribe to the Tuesday edition of *Newsday* and read my weekly book reviews." I closed with a cold "Sincerely" and signed my full name.

My most devoted fans, whom I had come to think of as "The Two," wrote back.

> Dear Florence:
> Thanks so much for your suggestion regarding the Tuesday *Newsday*. (How would you like to review *our* newest book: *Obsessions With a Failed Southern Lady?*!)
> We have just learned that we are able to take mutual vacation time and would like very much to spend about four days in the D.C. and Virginia area. We thought it would be fun to take a self-guided tour of some of the following places:
> —your birthplace at Park Road
> —Meridian Hill Park
> —the Mount Pleasant Branch Library
> —Congressional Cemetery
> —1020 Monroe Street
> —Raymond Elementary School
> —Powell Junior High School
> —the house Granny inherited
> —Fredericksburg
> We will, of course, arrange for our own lodging and transportation. We are considering mak-

ing our trip during one of the following time periods: [dates listed]. This tour that we are planning is not meant in any way to obligate you, Florence, although we would be delighted if you find that you would like to join us in our visit to any of these landmark locations! *It is never our intent to invade your privacy in any way,* and as your Fan Club representatives, it would indeed be a pleasure to, at the least, treat you to dinner.

Please let us know if any of the suggested dates sound convenient to you, or if an alternate time would suit your schedule better. Our real goal in all of this is to meet you, Florence. However, if, for any reason, you are unable to accept our dinner invitation, we will gladly postpone our trip until a better time unfolds. You've been so sweet to respond to us in your very personal way.

Bless your ever lovin' heart. . . .

I went into a panicky fury. The trite analogy about fighting mist or an unseen monster is too on-target for me to strive for anything more original to describe how I felt. Nothing is more frightening than being confronted by relentless contradiction. The repeated vows not to obligate me or invade my privacy, followed by stated intentions to do just that; the lavish adoration juxtaposed with arm-twisting hostility, seemed like an attack on rationality itself.

I began getting a lot of hang-up phone calls and suspected The Two were dialing my number just to hear my voice on the answering machine, though in view of their proven boldness it seemed more likely that they would say something . . . didn't it? I began sifting and weighing and analyzing everything, and actually used the dreadful phrase, "worst-case scenario," for the first time as I tried to anticipate what was going to happen next.

If I did not answer their letter they might take my silence for consent and go ahead with their trip. I would find them camped on my doorstep. Suppose they came to Fredericksburg and followed me around? Refused to leave? How would I get rid of them? Suppose they were crazy? They had already shown themselves to be precariously balanced between love and hate. Suppose they tilted hateside and pulled a gun on me? You don't have to be paranoid to think such things—just American.

Living through an extended period of mental tension affects different people in different ways. With me, release takes the form of giddy, cackling mischief. It occurred to me that if The Two carried out their plan to make a pilgrimage to my old D.C. neighborhood, my problem would be most efficaciously solved. I grew up in the section that was burned down during the Martin Luther King riots. The 14th Street of my childhood with its segregated dimestore lunch counters is now known as the Combat Zone; the Park Road of my birth is now lined with crack houses; and Meridian Hill Park, where Mama took me in my stroller, has been renamed for Malcolm X.

All I had to do was wait, and the Brothers would rescue me from my dilemma. Moreover, it would be the book-promotion coup of the century, the stuff that Jacqueline Susann's dreams were made of, something not even Irving Mansfield would dare try to arrange: two bodies found at 14th and Park Road with autographed copies of *Confessions of a Failed Southern Lady* clutched in their lifeless hands.

It was all but guaranteed that two lone white women roaming around such a neighborhood would get into serious trouble. When I thought more about it my mischief receded. Since they obviously knew nothing about Washington I felt it was my responsibility to warn them, but I couldn't do it without getting myself in deeper. They would interpret my warning as loving concern and be encouraged. For my own sake, I would have to stand by and do nothing while they walked into a trap.

That did it. . . .

The knowledge that they were preventing me from Doing Right (I can be *such* a shit) was the last straw. I detonated into a towering rage. Ignoring the possibility that I was dealing with psychopaths, I fired off what is known in certain quarters of the publishing world as "one of Florence's letters."

Dear Miss _____ and Miss _____:

I thought the formal tone of my reply to your request for family photos would be hint enough, but I see from your last letter that I shall have to be blunt.

Unlike many writers, I have always made a point of answering my fan mail because I consider my readers sacred. You, however, have overstepped the bounds and taken advantage of my good manners.

I find your familiarity offensive. I never address strangers by their first names and I don't permit them to so address me.

I find your persistence childish and obtuse.

I find what you call your "obsession" with me neurotic and repugnant.

I leave you with a quotation from Raymond Chandler that you would do well to study: "If you loved a book, don't meet the author."

They replied in two separate notes. Both opened with "Dear Miss King." Each woman apologized in the most abject manner, with words like "humble" and "beg." Clearly I had won, but it was a pyrrhic victory. Aggression turned to supineness, boldness turned to timidity, presumption turned to deference were but the other side of the coin. I was still on the receiving end of behavioral extremes.

Spoiled by so many years of excellent relations with my readers, I had to figure out what went wrong this time. I watched Lauren Bacall as the beset Broadway star in *The Fan* and read a book about John Lennon, but they shed little light because they did not seem to apply to me. Writers have always had a better class of fans than pop singers and sex symbols. It was performing artists who attracted the nuts. Writers were different.

"Not any more," said the writer friend I consulted. "This is the age of the book tour. We're all performing artists now."

Her theory turned up in a recent book, *Who Am I This Time? Uncovering the Fictive Personality* by Jay Martin.

In traditional societies, says Martin, individuals are shaped by three groups: 1) the people they actually know; 2) totemic figures such as gods, saints or ancestors; and 3) the people they do not know but meet through song and story, as the ancient Greeks met their mythological figures. In today's world, however, the second and third groups are provided by the media, so that celebrities have become the modern equivalents of the sacred and profane intercessors that provided unity and stability in former times.

I'm sure The Two had never seen me on television or they would have said so, but having no doubt seen other writers on talk shows, they were easily persuaded to worship me as a homegrown version of Hera crossed with Mollie Pitcher and Dolley Madison.

Simultaneously, however, they were urged toward the opposite emotion of familiarity by the studied folksiness of talk shows, which present celebrities chatting off the cuff in a mock-up living room. Thus they were able to divest me of the writer's traditional remoteness and regard me as a performing artist who had "come into their homes."

By sending the contradictory message that the famous are just plain folks on Mount Olympus, America has forged a relentless tension between loftiness and accessibility. Stir in the fact that the inborn talent and intelligence needed to achieve fame are immune to redistributive tinkering by government programs, and you have a definition of fame certain to produce envious rage: somebody screwed democracy.

Everybody's gotta right to be famous, however, so when all else fails you can become a celebrity by murdering one. "They can gas me but I am famous," said Sirhan Sirhan after shooting Robert Kennedy. "I am now a household word," said John Hinckley as he signed autographs for St. Elizabeth Hospital workers after shooting Ronald Reagan. Resentment of obscurity is so great, Jay Martin suggests, that skinheads may be drawn to Nazism not out of politics, but because they feel a personal identification with Hitler, who was described by George Wallace's assailant, Arthur Bremer, as "an unimportant, common person who rose to eminence."

The subject of fame is so ubiquitous that it emerged in Fawn Hall's first public utterance in her first press conference, in answer to the first question: "How do you feel?" Flashing a grin, tossing her mane, she replied: "A friend told me that Andy Warhol said everybody should be famous for fifteen minutes, so I guess it's my turn." There was no sense of cynicism or irony in her reply. It was clear that she was delighted by her sudden, undeserved fame, and equally clear that she expected it to be permanent—an expectation that was justified by the thought that ran through the heads of millions of viewers when she flashed that first grin: *She'd better get that tooth capped.*

America's fame problem makes sense in the light of one of my angel mother's inimitable phrases. When as a child I raised my voice in song, Mama would say, "You can't sing slop up a dark alley."

Mama was "supportive" (she called it backing me up) only to a certain point. That point was reality. I could read, I could write, I could spell "like a sonofabitch," as she proudly put it, but I couldn't sing and that was that.

Would that Mama and her vaudeville hook were with us still. Much of the ambivalence and hostility directed toward today's celebrities springs from the fact that a great many of them don't deserve to be celebrities. The country is full of famous people who can't sing slop up a dark alley, can't act slop up a dark alley, can't write slop up a dark alley, and they're all on television.

The spurious singers provide the most obvious example. I never watch their shows and movies but as a baseball fan I am unavoidably exposed to them when I watch the opening day game, the All-Star game, the playoffs, and the World Series—the games at which someone "sings" the national anthem.

The someone is nearly always a pop star whose name means nothing to me, so I can't document these remarks precisely, but I know what I know: I might not be able to sing myself but my problem lies in my voice, not my ear. These "singers" could not drive a plague wagon through a medieval street without going flat on "Bring out your dead!" Their tortuous efforts, especially those ululating moans designed to cover mistakes, make me more tense than loaded bases in the bottom of the ninth.

Will they make it? Will they crack? If they hit the low note in *say*, will they be able to reach the high one in *free*?

No one seems to care because a great many of these famous someones are sultry girls with lots of hair whose real talent consists of performing fellatio on the mike. While she struggles and strains, most of the players fidget and blow bubblegum; here and there in the stands one sees a patriot, usually an old man, standing at attention, but most of the spectators eat, drink, and talk until "The Star-Spangled Banner" blessedly comes to an end.

Many pundits have condemned the disrespect shown the national anthem at such times, but they never make the connection between the disrespect and the quality of the rendition. It has nothing to do with patriotism. It is simply a human reaction to mediocrity.

Each time a mediocre singer performs he is saying, in effect, "This is good enough for you." The audience, thrust into that familiar American mood of knowing that something is wrong but not knowing what it is, unconsciously absorbs the insult and projects it back onto the mediocre performer in the form of inattention, rudeness, and noise.

The human spirit craves excellence. It's the performer's gift to his public that paves a two-way street: an excellent performance says, in effect, "I respect you enough to justify your respect for me." Being in the presence of excellence brings out the best in people; looking up is better moral exercise than looking level or down, but with mediocrity riding shotgun on the stagecoach of national life, American popular entertainment offers little in the way of spiritual aerobics.

Having too many celebrities and not enough excellence makes it impossible to tell who deserves respect and who does not—hence "The Look" that accompanied

"*I saw you on television*" on the faces of the family in the station wagon, and the familiarity, presumption, and ambivalent adoration of The Two.

America could come to terms with fame if we viewed it through the prism of karmic law. When a person is given a talent by the gods, he is obligated to give it back to the world. If he fails to do so, or does so half-heartedly, he is in breach of the metaphysical contract and will be punished in his next life in a manner befitting his crime.

The painter who abandons or corrupts his talent will come back blind, the musician will come back deaf, and the writer will come back mentally retarded. As for the woman who gives up a career in the creative arts for marriage and motherhood, I believe such a decision places her in a state comparable to what Christianity calls mortal sin: she had the talent before she had the family. (This was Sylvia Plath's problem. Her madness and suicide resulted from what was essentially a religious crisis: she tried to serve two masters.)

You don't have to be into Eastern religions to appreciate the awesome respect for talent inherent in karmic thinking. By contrast, Americans respect talent only insofar as it leads to fame, and we reserve our most fervent admiration for famous people who destroy their lives as well as their talent. The fatal flaws of Elvis, Judy, and Marilyn register much higher on our national applause meter than their living achievements. In America, talent is merely a tool for becoming famous in life so you can become more famous in death—where all are equal.

THE SILVER
SCREAM

As one born in 1936, I am a member of America's most
movie-influenced generation, raised on the great films
of Hollywood's golden age.

Children of the thirties and forties went to the movies
every time the picture changed, which was two or three
times a week. In that era of non-working mothers and
live-in grandmothers, I would get home from school to
find Mama and Granny ready and waiting for our afternoon treat at the Tivoli, our neighborhood theater
at 14th and Park Road.

We never paid any attention to the schedule. The
idea was to go to the movies right after school let out so
we would be home in time for dinner. If we happened
to arrive when the picture was starting, fine; if not, that
was fine too. More often than not, we got in at the middle
just in time to see Miriam Hopkins burst into tears, or
Bette Davis shoot somebody, without having the faintest

idea why. We watched from the middle to the end, then saw the "selected short subjects," then the "previews of coming attractions," and finally, when the next continuous showing started, we saw the beginning.

Seeing movies backwards was not merely our family eccentricity, but a national practice. The catch phrase, "This is where I came in," originated at this time, though with three mindsets to deal with, we never could agree on when that was. Granny, a Victorian, remembered deathbed scenes; Mama, an unregenerate tomboy, noticed fights and cars; and I was in the animal-loving stage when children want to grow up to be veterinarians.

"We got here when she fell off the horse."

"No, we didn't *see* her fall off, we just heard the doctor say she was paralyzed for life while we were buying popcorn."

"George Raft was beating somebody up when we sat down."

"Oh, look, there's Charles Coburn with his head in his hands! *That's* where we came in."

If it wasn't too late, remaining to see a favorite scene over again was also common practice, with the child as arbiter: "I wanna see her fall off the horse again."

The movie theaters of the era were rightly called "palaces." The lush dream of romance and adventure in faraway places began when we bought our tickets from a cashier seated in an ornate box modeled on a Turkish caliph's sedan chair.

Inside, the theater was an opulent cave with thick carpeting and a sweeping marble staircase leading to the balcony. The walls of the auditorium were covered in plush brocade; I remember pushing my small fist against it and marveling that it yielded like a pillow. The brocade was shot with gilded thread in whose whorls I saw other pictorial dramas of my own imagining—a pirate, a lady in a big hat, a prancing horse—just as I did when I lay in bed at home and looked up at the paintbrush marks on the ceiling. But these images were more ingratiating because they emerged from luxuriant silk instead of plain white plaster.

When the movie ended and the soft amber lights came up, the magic remained. No one moved for a moment; staying seated quietly in the cool penumbra was a gentle transition the audience could not resist. Finally, with what seemed like a collective sigh, people rose and walked slowly up the aisle, stumbling a little from the combined effects of the spongy carpet and the lingering daze of enchantment.

The spell was not broken until we left the theater and emerged onto the street. My first attack of depression came on a sizzling afternoon in September. What struck me was the contrast—the unbearably sudden contrast between dark and light; between air-conditioned chill and heat-baked sidewalks; between the storybook vistas of the movie just seen and the stark reality of tawdry, noisy 14th Street.

A lump formed in my throat. I wanted to cry but I didn't dare. I knew from experience what would happen. My combative mother would have jumped to her favorite conclusion and demanded, "Did somebody at school pick on you? Why didn't you beat the shit out of them?" While Mama was getting all worked up, Granny, who wanted me to be a delicate Southern lady, would have chimed in with, "The child isn't well." It was easier to keep my troubles to myself, so I did.

The depression receded once we got home and back into our usual routine, but the memory of it remained with me. I kept thinking about the contrast, which I called "the different." Not the different light, or the different temperature, just *The Different*, as in a Stephen King title.

Over the next several weeks, it happened each time

we left the theater. Although I managed not to cry on the street, ultimately I did something worse: I broke down in the crowded ladies' lounge of the Tivoli.

Many years later when I went to Versailles, all I could think of was that ladies' lounge. They were furnished the same way; Louis Quinze chairs, tables, and settees, ornate gilded mirrors, curlicued gilded frames containing pictures of Fragonard courtiers chasing nymphs through sylvan glades.

But the lounge contained something that Versailles did not: ashtrays. Tall, tubular, stainless steel receptacles like umbrella stands, filled with sand and stuck with lipstick-smeared butts. There was one beside each Louis Quinze settee. The contrast between the modern, gleaming steel containers and the kind of furniture I had so often seen in costume movies was too much. Past and present, reality and fantasy, movie and life, were side by side, next to each other, *touching*.

I started crying.

"What's the matter?" asked Granny.

"Jesus Christ on roller skates!" Mama, of course.

"Oh, the poor little thing," some woman quavered.

"Did the movie scare you, honey?" asked another.

"It's those cartoons," said a third. "They're supposed to be funny but everybody gets run over by steamrollers."

"Did somebody at school pick on you?"

"The poor little thing, she reminds me of Margaret O'Brien in that movie—oh, what was the name of that? You remember, when she cried and cried and cried?"

"What's the matter?" Granny asked again.

"I don't know!" I sobbed. "It's the different!"

"What's different?"

"The ashtrays! They make me sad! I can't stand them!"

"Jesus Christ on roller skates! Who do you think you are, Greta Garbo?"

Despite the stark reality I was pumping into the atmosphere, even my down-to-earth mother drew on the movies for her shouted analogy. The woman across the lounge was still more captive to fantasy; she had forgotten all about me and was back in the Margaret O'Brien movie.

"It was about the war and she was an orphan in London and Robert Young wanted to adopt her but something happened that he couldn't and then she just started crying and crying and crying. She wore a little peaked cap like a gremlin and wouldn't let go of her telescope, and I think somebody died. Was it Loretta Young? Anyhow, she just kept crying and crying and crying like her poor little heart would break. Oh, *what* was the name of that?"

"The child isn't well," Granny decreed.

On that note we left. By the time we got home, she had remembered a distant cousin "who was never well," and spent the rest of the evening sighing, "It runs in the family." I had to spend the rest of the evening convincing Mama that nobody had picked on me.

Maybe it was knowing that I had played into their hands that helped me pull myself together. Maybe my public crying jag had drained me of pity and terror. Maybe children are emotionally resilient. Or maybe it was simply because I loathed Margaret O'Brien. For whatever reason, The Different never returned after that.

Everyone quickly forgot about it. Mama shrugged it off with her all-purpose explanation—"You're deep, just like your father"—and Granny shortly got interested in something else that ran in the family. For my part, ever eager to dissociate myself from the genus children and fiercely proud of puffs like *mature for her age* and *beyond her years* that my teachers wrote on my report cards, I decided that The Different was the last vestige of childhood, the emotional counterpart of my last skinned knee.

I was wrong. It came back again and again throughout my life, albeit in subtler ways. Nor did I suffer alone. The Different is America's eternal, universal emotion; it stays with us for life and attacks everybody except the Amish because the only way to avoid it is never to go to the movies.

My childhood version of The Different was like Emily Dickinson's "certain slant of light," a simple revulsion against abrupt contrast. Being a city child who wanted to live in a country house like the ones in *Wuthering Heights* and *Kings Row*, the grinding streetcars and sun-baked sidewalks were sudden, unbearable reminders of where I did live. Later, as an adult, I came to like cities, but by then I was susceptible to another kind of post-movie depression.

There is more sexism in a year's worth of movies than actually exists in a woman's entire lifetime. The movies of the fifties and early sixties were constant reminders that every inclination I had was wrong. Close-ups of babies had to be greeted with "Awwwww," not the "Uggghhh" I was thinking. The contemptuous hoots that greeted the sexually erring woman and the casting-office spinster in hornrim glasses filled me with angry confusion. In a contrary way I wanted to be both women, and somehow I sensed that I would be both.

Countless scripts called for the female star to deliver some version of the ringing line, "I just want to be a *woman!*" When Eleanor Parker as opera star Marjorie Lawrence gave up her career to marry Glenn Ford, silencing his protests with, "I've *had* all that! I just want to be Mrs. Thomas King!" the audience burst into applause that sent me into a cringing sulk.

By the time the show was over I felt like a stainless steel ashtray next to a Louis Quinze settee: instead of suffering from The Different, I had become it.

The post-movie mood is more often than not a bad one. How many arguments have you had or heard on leaving the theater? The young woman suddenly snaps at her date after spending two hours with Charlton Heston or Robert Redford. The husband still under the spell of the French Foreign Legion suddenly yells at the wife and kids who are keeping him from a life of adventure. The child emerging from *My Friend Flicka* gets slapped because he keeps whining "Why can't we go live on a ranch?" The wife who has just seen *Gaslight* goes wild when her husband says he can't find the car keys, and the two middle-aged women who have just seen *Mildred Pierce* together can't wait to get home and give their daughters hell.

Mama and I had an awful fight the night we went to see *To Catch a Thief*. I was then about the same age as the Grace Kelly character. I smelled trouble during the show when Jessie Royce Landis, who played Kelly's rip-snortin' mother, said: "My daughter's ashamed of me." My own rip-snortin' mother grunted and leaned as far away from me as she could get, so what happened later in the parking lot came as no surprise.

"I guess you're ashamed of me, huh? Because I don't speak French, huh? Shit on French!" she bellowed, banging her fist on the hood. "Shit on you! I'm as good as you are, you little snot, so take your French and shove it!" Some people a few cars over burst into applause.

It was what screenwriters aim for: Mama had "identified" with a character. I had not; I didn't like Grace Kelly but I did identify with one of her lines: "The only

difference between Mother and me is a little grammar."
I found it very touching because it was a perfect description of Mama and me, but when I tried to tell her
this, she refused to believe it. A movie had come between
us, and I wondered how many others had. What did she
feel when she saw *Stella Dallas*? Did that hurt her too?

I like to imagine how pleasant and confident life
would be if movies had never been invented. An insig-
nificant mishap like a crumbled wine cork would not
make a man feel like an unsophisticated clod because
he never would have seen Cary Grant extract one with
a single adroit twist. With no one to imitate, everyone
would have his own bona fide personality, and it would
be a stronger one for being real. We would not be burdened with our current "crisis in self-esteem" because
untold millions of people would not have spent the last
seven decades walking off into the night brooding, "If
only I could look like that . . . dance like that . . . swim
like that." And we would be free of the kind of sheer
idiocy that makes people set their hearts on owning a
car whose doors close with a whooshy *snick*! because it's
the "rich car door sound" they heard in movies.

Whenever I speculate on what women would be like
had movies never been invented, I need look no further
than Granny. Thirty-six in 1915 when *Birth of a Nation*
and Theda Bara's *A Fool There Was* inaugurated the
movie era, her personality was formed long before Hollywood encouraged women to exchange identity for
identification.

By the time I knew her, she got to the movies at least
twice a week, but the movies never got to her. Her favorite scenes involved sickbeds and terminal illness, but
her reaction was that of a technical adviser rather than
a hypnotized spectator in the throes of romantic masochism. Old enough and rural enough to have witnessed
real home deaths from a variety of grim causes, she was

60

unimpressed when Jennifer Jones swallowed arsenic in *Madame Bovary*.

"You never look that pretty when you're full of arsenic," she whispered to me. "I'll never forget the time Willie Codrick swallowed the rat poison. He was spewing like a fountain—from *both* ends."

Obsessive love moved her not. "The worse you treat a man, the better he treats you," she whispered during *Letter From an Unknown Woman*. "The *man* should be the one who's in love," she advised throughout *Back Street*. Equally lost on her were hankering dissatisfaction and hopeless yearning. Her resolute contentment was never more in evidence than when we went to see Bette Davis in *Beyond the Forest*.

There was Davis as nostril-flaring Rosa Moline, married to good, dull Joseph Cotten, stuck in a small town and a shabby house ("What a dump!") that she hates. Consumed by the desire to run away to Chicago, her eyes stretch open every time she hears the train whistle. Bosom heaving in frustration, she gazes in the direction of Chicago and then paces, paces, paces like a caged animal while the background music plays "Chicago, Chicago."

Finding herself pregnant, she throws herself down a hill to get rid of the baby who is keeping her from fleeing to Chicago. Dying of blood poisoning from the botched miscarriage, she drags herself out of bed and crawls on her hands and knees through the town to the railroad station while the background music plays a labored version of "Chicago, Chicago." As she collapses on the platform and claws the air, the Chicago train pulls in and momentarily hides her from view. When it pulls out again, we see her lying dead as the background music plays "Chicago, Chicago" in funeral-march time.

The women seated around us were clutching their throats and moaning "Oh, no, no!" Mama was sitting forward in her seat and I, too young to appreciate Rosa's problems but knowing real tragedy when I saw it, was drooling soggy popcorn from a corner of my open mouth.

"Why would anybody want to go to Chicago?" Granny asked irritably. "It's full of Yankees."

THE GRAVES
OF ACADEME

For years I have had a recurring dream about quitting college. I see my youthful self walking across the campus toward a classroom building. Suddenly I stop and stand motionless in the middle of the quadrangle, overcome by a realization that makes me feel like an inventor who has stumbled upon a brilliant yet simple discovery. "I don't *have* to do this," I say, "I don't *have* to be here." I turn abruptly and walk out through the college gates, bathed in an ecstasy so intense that it wakes me up.

This is not the dream of a mediocre student for whom academic work was an anxiety-provoking struggle. I won a scholarship to American University in Washington, D.C. and graduated with honors in 1957 with a double major in history and English. Since I was qualified to do nothing except go to graduate school, I applied for and won a fellowship in history at the University of Mississippi.

I completed the course work for the M.A. but did not finish my thesis because I found something better to do. I spent the entire spring semester writing stories for the true confessions magazines. After turning out footnoted reams on such pressing topics as the annexation of Schleswig-Holstein and the reign of Pippin the Short, I got five cents a word for "I Committed Adultery in a Diabetic Coma" and it felt *great*. I had thrown off the vague guilt of the welfare scholar and become a productive member of society at last.

I have been getting paid for writing ever since but this chapter is the only piece of writing I've ever done that required a college education. If I could be transported back in time to my high school graduation, I would not go to college. I would turn down the scholarship, get a proofreading job with a printer, and write on evenings and weekends.

As for "cultural literacy," I would acquire it the only way it can be acquired: by reading. Reading. . . . what Americans pay colleges to let them do. Reading. . . . what colleges pay scholarship students to do. Reading. . . . what I have been doing compulsively since the age of six and would have gone on doing through hell and high water anyway.

America's love affair with college that got me off the track thirty-five years ago has now flowered into an obsession so widespread that politicians invoke it as they once invoked motherhood. During the Congressional pay-raise flap, those who favored the increase explained plangently that they needed the money "to send our kids to college," and Chief Justice William H. Rehnquist called a press conference to plead for a raise for federal judges "so they can educate their kids."

Parents are destroying their health and mortgaging their homes to pay for their children's college education. (These are the same parents who don't want to be a "burden" on their children in their old age.) Millions of women long since disenchanted with feminism who secretly want to stay home and be housewives, and whose families could get along on one paycheck under normal conditions, are working at jobs they hate so they can help send their children to college.

Millions of other women who quit college the first time around because they caught the husband that they went to college to catch are now going back to college to cure what feminists call "lack of self-esteem." Fear of not going to college is so great that McDonald's has become a metaphor for failure: if you don't get a degree, warn the experts, you will spend the rest of your life flipping hamburgers for the minimum wage.

What is behind our college lust? How did we get buried alive in this grave of academe?

As with most other American problems, the joker in the deck is democracy. When we abolished titles of rank and launched a classless society, everyone immediately tried to figure out a way to wriggle free of the official idealism and be superior in spite of it all. At first it was "go into business for yourself" and "be your own boss," which created a quintessential American type, the self-made man who bragged about how dumb he was in that ringing statement, "I only went to the eighth grade."

A well like this was bound to run dry, and when it did we conceived the idea of the self-made college graduate who "worked his way through college." His success enabled him to reach another social plateau, that of "being able to send his children to college." The children went, and had so much fun that Betty Coed and Joe College made the 1920s roar.

The contemporaries of Betty and Joe who didn't go to college started to feel inferior, so that when their sons came home from World War II and found the GI Bill of Rights waiting to pay their tuition, they told them:

"Don't be like us, make something of yourself, go to college." The presence on the nation's campuses of so many millions of eligible bachelors inspired what was tactfully called "higher education for women," and the notorious "MrS. degree" of the fifties was born.

Aiding and abetting all of the above has been the fact that the two major societal influences in our national life are both tied up with education. One is the immigrant experience, the "better than" syndrome that calls on each generation to advance one step up the ladder.

The other is the Anglo-Saxon dear-old-golden-rule-days syndrome of school as nostalgia. Read the memoirs of famous Englishmen and you will find lugubriously sentimental tributes to the playing fields of Eton, dear old Chips, good old Bunny, the crew, and the team, but rarely is there any mention of learning. In America this attitude has translated into the Wasp big-man-on-campus syndrome personified by Dan Quayle. It defines college as a place to be well-rounded in—*i.e.*, you're supposed to hate books but love school.

With all of us impaled on this two-pronged stake there is probably no way to end America's college lust, but I would nonetheless like to offer some warnings. Rather than recite statistics, I will confine myself to personal experiences and observations.

1. College is increasingly becoming a place to die in. The widespread "Why am I here?" depression that strikes in senior year more often results in suicide than in the sensible decision of my recurring dream. The more people who go to college for the wrong reasons —greed, guilt, or dreams of status—the more such suicides there will be.

2. By encouraging great expectations in ordinary people in a not-so-great economy, college produces what George Bernard Shaw called "downstarts"—people

whose dreams don't pan out, who form an envious, resentful, discontented mass far more dangerous than any proletarian mob.

Some excellent candidates for the ivy-covered barricades are the children of Jon Hilliard of Indiana, who stated in the April 24, 1989 issue of *Time*: "I grew up in a poor family with four kids, and we had no extras. There's no way my kids are going to be like that. We want to make sure that if they're not good athletes *or smart academically*, they can still go to college." [my italics]

3. College creates passive people. Speaking on the subject of adult education, Anthony Trollope said: "It is so difficult for a man to go back to the verdure and malleability of pupildom, who has once escaped from the necessary humility of its conditions." All college education is adult education; keeping so many young adults in school from eighteen to twenty-one and beyond trains them to be subordinate, ingratiating, anxious-to-please toadies.

4. College teaching tends to attract the kind of people who are incapable of making a living with either their minds or their hands. If I had children I would rather turn them over to a capable shop foreman or top sergeant than most of the college teachers I've met.

The sheer goofiness of many professors is especially evident at faculty parties, the best description of which is found in Philip Lee Williams's new novel, *The Song of Daniel*: "The party, like all academic parties, was like riding down a grocery store aisle in a cart with a flat wheel."

A writer living in a college town has to take extreme steps to avoid faculty parties. At the last one I attended I overheard a member of the English Department say, in what passes for chit-chat at these fêtes: "Dogs were not generally well-thought of in late Renaissance England." I thought to myself: *Well, goddamn. . . . How did I ever get along without knowing that? Now I can go on through this vale of tears called life, armed with the inestimable knowledge of what late Renaissance England thought of dogs.*

That was the night I took extreme steps. In a discussion of the relative merits of George Bush and Michael Dukakis, I said, "What this country needs is Principal Joe Clark. He walks fast and carries a baseball bat." I haven't been invited back since.

For female students especially, college teachers are mad, bad, and dangerous to know. The average faculty is full of adult male tittybabies who do nothing but harm, with that pipe-smoking sonofabeech, the Sensuous Professor, leading the list.

In the pantheon of male chauvinist piggery, the academic male is a wart hog with the personality traits of a harem eunuch. Ingratiating and devious from his obsessive pursuit of tenure, anxious and irritable from his publish-or-perish labors, and burdened with the image of the great American indoorsman, he proves his masculinity in nasty, supercilious, underhanded ways that are much more infuriating than the "me Tarzan-you Jane" upfrontness of good ole boys.

A paradigmatic example of this trait can be found on the acknowledgements page of a book called *Pursuing the American Dream: White Ethnics and the New Populism* by Richard Krickus:

> Most of all, my wife Mary Ann deserves special mention. She spent long hours conducting research for this book, provided incisive editorial comments, and frequently challenged the author's ideas and biases with enthusiasm and intelligence. If it were not for certain flaws in the author's character, her name would accompany his on the title page.

5. College as conscience is an especially insidious American game that has lured millions into a hypocritical cop-out. "Enlightened" people are free of prejudice, goes the argument, so send everybody to college and let education do what character ought. The end result has been not enlightenment but a sly freemasonry among college graduates that assumes we all hold "correct" political opinions, which effectively discourages any frank discussion of the problems that our education supposedly equips us to solve.

6. Do you know what your children are studying in college? At one Virginia college they are studying me. A class in "communications"—whatever that is—is reading *Confessions of a Failed Southern Lady*. I'm not indulging in false modesty; it's a good book and I'm proud of it, but it's the kind of book you read for pleasure *after* you finish your homework assignments in Tolstoy and Austen. Too many snap courses like this, and too many papers on—God help us all—"Symbolic Undercurrents in Florence King" are why we are increasingly becoming a nation of ignoramuses.

7. As the only class distinction available in a democracy, the college degree has created a caste society as rigid as ancient India's. Condemning elitism and simultaneously quaking in fear that our children won't become members of the elite, we send them to college not to learn, but to "be" college graduates, rationalizing our snobbery with the cliché that high technology has eliminated the need for the manual labor that we secretly hold in contempt.

Only an American labor leader would say, as Samuel Gompers did: "The promise of America for the laboring man is the promise of someday no longer having to work with his hands." We are paying through the nose for such attitudes. If you can't get your car fixed properly it may well be because your mechanic is crippled by "lack of self-esteem" because he didn't go to college, or because his mind is on his night-school course at the community college, or because he's so exhausted from trying to pay his children's tuition that he can't tell a carburetor from a fan belt—or because he wants to get even with the people who look down on him by screwing up their cars.

Our attitude toward non-college people bespeaks a criminal disregard of their feelings and their worth. By our insane efforts to transform the entire population into an educated middle class, we are tempting the fate described by Oliver Goldsmith in his famous lines: *"A bold peasantry, their country's pride, when once destroyed, can never be supplied."*

If we keep shoving everybody into college we will end as a nation of white-collar nervous Nellies without true culture or purpose, living in dread of McDonald's and tapping away at our high-tech machines while the "underclass" that didn't even finish high school seethes at our backs.

Nowadays we prefer to keep quiet about people who make it big without going to college. Should the truth emerge anyway, we try to find something wrong with them. We wait eagerly to see if they will turn out to be like Henry Ford: anti-Semitic idiot savants who took a "tragic" fork in the road because of "gaps" in their education.

Try as we might to stop it, however, the cream still rises to the top of the bottle. A shining example of non-college success is Edna Buchanan, Pulitzer Prize-winning crime reporter on the *Miami Herald*, whose memoir, *The Corpse Had a Familiar Face*, appeared a couple of years ago.

After her father abandoned them, Edna and her mother lived in a rat-infested Paterson, New Jersey, tenement. "College was obviously out of the question and was never discussed," she says. "It was simply understood that I would work full time after high school."

After a stint as a dimestore salesgirl, she got a job at the Western Electric factory and worked alongside her mother wiring switchboards. When they moved to Miami, Edna, who had always been a compulsive reader, applied for and got a job as society reporter on a small Miami Beach paper after confessing to the managing editor that she had never gone to college or studied journalism. "Good," he said, "you won't have to unlearn anything."

When she switched to the *Herald*'s police beat, she brought to her bloodcurdling assignments the kind of vivid writing that cannot be taught.

Covering the death of an unqualified Haitian immigrant hired by a textile factory, she writes: "Working alone, overnight, he had to make sure that no threads caught, that nothing snarled the works. The next morning they found him tangled in the machinery—knitted to death."

Or this karate-chop description of "body packers"— drug smugglers from Bolivia who swallow condom-wrapped cocaine and get on a plane to Miami: "They die in lonely hotel rooms with a fortune they can't touch in their gut."

Or this: "A man trying to murder his wife pumped fifty gallons of propane gas into their house, then positioned himself on the front steps and reached into the door with a lighted match. Police arrived and found a vacant lot."

Buchanan's literary style springs not from creative writing courses but from an ear for rhythm and sound, like an ear for music, that is present in the genes; and

71

an eye for word pictures that might have made her a painter had her parents' sperm and egg done something a little differently. Why creative talent turns up in some but not others is one of the few mysteries left, but any geneticist who wishes to pursue the matter should start with Edna Buchanan.

I had the privilege of working with a legendary woman who did not go to college. Gloria Safier, who died in 1985, was the last of the old-warhorse literary agents. The daughter of a movie distributor, she liked to say, "My math was the gross in Cleveland." When the father deserted the family, his wife and two daughters fell upon hard times, so Gloria graduated from Erasmus Hall High School in Brooklyn and the next day went to work as a gofer for Billy Rose.

After a stint on the Coast as assistant to Myron Selznick, she returned to New York, borrowed four thousand dollars, and opened her own theatrical agency. The loan was soon repaid; her triumphs included winning for the unknown Wally Cox the title role in the wildly popular early television sitcom, "Mr. Peepers."

Gloria never used the vocabulary of literary criticism to make her points. When more indirection was called for, she would bark, "You don't have to draw a picture!" If you resolved a plot with a deus ex machina, she would call up and growl, "Where the hell did that Johnny-on-the-spot come from?" And if you skimped on foreshadowing, you could count on being jarred out of sleep by an eight a.m. phone call: "Didn't your mother ever teach you how to hint?"

Although she made millions for and from intellectuals, she never felt insecure in their presence and invariably saw through their pretenses. Arlene Francis tells the story of the time she took a reluctant Gloria to see the deep, dark problem play, *Rosencrantz and Guildenstern Are Dead*. Gloria obediently sat through it, seeming for once to behave herself, but when the lights came up after the final act, she turned to Arlene Francis, pointed to the title on the program and said: "What did I tell you?"

So much for high school graduates. Georgia-born memoirist and poet Rosemary Daniell quit high school at sixteen to get married, but her description of a failed Southern belle enroute to madness brings this college graduate to my knees in reverence:

> Every dresser drawer reflected the chaos of her psyche. Broken lipsticks, empty compacts, beads spilled from broken necklaces mingled with the powder drifting from round pink Pond's boxes, overdue bills, curling family photographs, recipes clipped from *Good Housekeeping*, imprinted repeatedly by her lips. When I was fourteen, Mother screamed that she had found a mouse nursing her young in one of the drawers; as we gathered around to look at the pink flesh fingertips, the cringing gray mother, it only seemed that Mother's mess had finally spawned life. Everywhere, her hysteria made literal metaphors.

I was raised by two *junior* high dropouts and two elementary school dropouts, but all four of them were well-educated people.

My British father "left school" at fifteen according to the custom of his time and class, yet he could recite the major speeches of Shakespeare and the monarchs of England, with dates, from Alfred the Great.

My baseball-crazed mother quit school at fourteen and never read a book (including mine) in her life, but she could compute batting averages in a trice, and when we went grocery shopping she added up the prices in her head and arrived at the same total, at the same time, as the cash register.

My grandmother had six years of school in rural Virginia but she learned enough to be able to turn herself into a self-taught archivist, able to find the public documents she needed to trace our family back to 1672.

Jensy, our black cleaning woman, went to school for only a couple of years, yet she read the Bible straight through every year and once pointed out an incorrect statement about the Kingdom of Babylon in my ancient history textbook.

How many current college graduates are capable of doing *any* of these things?

What can we do about one notion, highly risible, a college education for all? Here we come to the conundrum I call "The Last Graf."

When you write critical articles for magazines, they always want a final, upbeat paragraph offering positive solutions for the problems you have identified. Given my outlook on life, a large chunk of my professional day consists of phone calls from editors that begin, "We love the piece, but you left something out."

The typical Last Graf always calls for "more education" on whatever God-awful American mess is under discussion, but since this essay is about the perils of too much education, I can't very well call for more.

Never let it be said, however, that I can't come up with a Last Graf. The liberals don't call me Ku Klux King for nothing, so here are my unthinkable solutions for dousing the fires of our college lust.

First, we must admit that most jobs do not require a college education. Let's stop referring to every white-collar job as a "profession." There are only three professions: medicine, law, and the clergy.

Practitioners of professions go it alone; they hang out a shingle and wait for people to come to them. They do not join labor unions or go on strike because they are motivated—or should be—not by mere interest or naked greed but by a "calling." Their income varies according to how much work they do; they do a certain amount of pro bono work in a spirit of noblesse oblige. They can be sued for malpractice, and they are bound by "professional privilege"—what goes on between them and their clients is secret and they cannot be made to reveal it.

Teaching is not a profession but a unionized government job loaded with benefits. Journalists are reporters, architects are builders, and writers are craftsmen—a run-on sentence to me is like an overlong table leg to a carpenter: I saw it off and sand it down.

Second, let's make our public schools so good that few people will need to go to college. I don't mean the usual nonsense we hear constantly, about "motivation" and "enrichment." I'm talking about radical change. We need to get rid of certain people who aren't worth the powder and shot to blow them to Kingdom Come. Specifically, teachers whose majors are in "Education"; their capos, the moronic professors of "Education"; and that empire-building collection of anti-intellectual pissants known as the National "Education" Association.

Once we replace the cretinous Educationists with real teachers, we should lengthen the school day to nine-to-five, the school year to eleven months; adopt a *national* curriculum emphasizing phonics in the early grades; reproduce the curriculum of the Boston Latin School, circa 1900, for junior and senior high; and put Joe Clark in charge of the whole business with no questions asked.

Of all the "czars" among us, he is the only one with a real Romanov touch.

Lengthened school hours would solve much of the day-care problem. Students unable or unwilling to keep up with high academic standards could quit school at the end of the sixth grade and still come out with a better basic education than that bestowed by today's worthless high school diploma. If we got rid of students like this in elementary school, we would need far fewer junior and senior high school teachers, and could therefore afford to pay this smaller number much higher salaries.

None of the foregoing has a snowball's chance, of course, but somebody had better come up with a Last Graf soon. If our educational standards fall any lower we will end up with the elitism we profess to dread. Only rich children who go to the best private schools will learn how to read and write. Literature will regress to private diary entries called "My Gleanings" like those penned by complacent Victorians on walking tours through Scotland, and novels will revert to a pre-Hardy treatment of the lower classes as villains and figures of comic relief.

We will also have even more crazies than we have now. The illiterate person is a touchy person. Hearing someone say "if I was," and then a few moments later "if I were," he thinks: *What's the difference? What's going on? They're making fun of me, that's what.* . . . . BANG!

Even as I write this, George Bush and the nation's governors are gathered in Charlottesville, Virginia to solve the Crisis in Education. It promises to be one of those frenetic American egg hunts known as "seeking answers" in which the answer that is staring everyone in the face is left to rot in the grass.

The word *education*, as Miss Jean Brodie liked to say, comes from a Greek root meaning "to draw out." Socrates made this point when he took an illiterate slave boy and, with deft questioning, got him to solve a complex mathematical problem by making him use knowledge that he did not know he had.

Deep-dish thinking will never catch on in America because the vast majority of our citizens are *Whatters*: people whose conversations consist of *what* they did, *what* they saw, *what* they bought, the kind of basic-nutrient talk that British writer Emlyn Williams called "monotonous but it keeps you going, the fish and chips of the mind."

Whyers drive them up the wall because we are always raising hypothetical questions and spinning them into theoretical discussions. Thus confronted, Whatters react in one of four ways. They reply, "You think too much!" and jab you in the ribs. They sputter, "Who cares?" and give an irritated snort. They adopt a position of moral superiority and say, "I don't *want* to know." Or they give an air-clearing wave and chortle, "Hey, the party's getting serious!" All four reactions are accompanied by the nervous look known as "askance" in respectable people and "shifty-eyed" in the other kind.

Whatters tend to fall into one of two gender groups, as college-trained sociologists would say. Most female Whatters are members of the subcategory Nice Women with LUV vanity plates and Year of the Child Christmas cards. Male Whatters are husbands ("You never talk to me!" "What would you like to talk about?") or blind dates ("You'd be a great gal if only you'd develop a sense of humor").

Whatters are extremely gregarious, which gives them a lot more people to talk about nothing with than Whyers ever have to talk about something with.

The only thing stronger than the Whatter's aversion

to thinking is his devotion to problem solving. His favorite recipe for dealing with traumatic emotions like grief is: "Keep busy so you won't have time to think." The Whatter way of combining this old saw with the modern demands of Resources 'n' Awareness is to take a course in Grief Management that meets three evenings a week from seven to nine at a suburban community college on the other side of the Beltway. At the end of the course, all the Whatters will have identical thoughts about grief and lots of new friends to discuss rush-hour traffic with.

Politically, Whatters are of the persuasion flatteringly known as Independent. Anyone who suggests, as Whyers are wont to do, that Independents are wind-testing conformists who can be swung like a lariat will be treated to the Whatter's favorite campaign slogan. It used to be "I vote for the man, not the party"; now it's "I vote for the person, not the party."

Whatters are enthusiastic voters because American political campaigns speak to their deepest instincts. ("What issues?") Anyone who wants the Whatter vote need only say, "I will be president of *all* the people." Whatters know that this promise effectively shuts out the Whyers of America, especially if the election is held on one of those days when half of us are hung over and the other half are back in the funny farm.

It must be said: Whatters built America. For every secretly tormented Thomas Jefferson nursing migraines, there were thousands of uncomplicated yeomen who said, "What's that?" and opened fire as soon as the bushes moved.

It must further be said: Whatters are by no means dumb. Many of them are as smart as the proverbial whip, as can be seen in this description of one of their leading prototypes:

But Scarlett intended to marry—and marry Ashley—and she was willing to appear demure, pliable and scatterbrained, if those were the qualities that attracted men. Just why men should be this way, she did not know. She only knew that such methods worked. It never interested her enough to try to think out the reason for it, for she knew nothing of the inner workings of any human being's mind, not even her own. She knew only that if she did or said thus-and-so, men would unerringly respond with the complementary thus-and-so. It was like a mathematical formula and no more difficult, for mathematics was the one subject that had come easy to Scarlett in her schooldays.

Scarlett had no understanding of Ashley's love of books, and no patience with his habit of ruminating. My mother, the smartest Whatter I have ever known, reacted the same way to my father's ruminations.

"Where is the past?" he asked one night at dinner. "What happens to it after it finishes being the present? Where does it go? It must go somewhere."

"Jesus Christ on rollerskates!"

As prejudiced as I am in favor of Whyers, it must be said: we also suck.

Many of my fellow Whyers are the very same pseudo-intellectual diddlysquats who perpetrated the progressive hoax, "Teach students not *what* to think but *how* to think." They did not mean required courses in logic because people who study logic might figure out too much. They meant staring at a photograph from *Erskine Caldwell's America* and writing down "what it makes me feel." They worship education but are embarrassed by knowledge—especially classical knowledge. Display the

79

slightest familiarity with Latin and they will accuse you of showing off.

Whyers also cause trouble with our eternal quest for the catchy phrase that will guarantee us entry into the quotations dictionary of some editor yet unborn. The lure of the parallelism got its start long before Jesse Jackson. Voltaire was striving for one when he said, "I may not agree with what you say but I will defend to the death your right to say it." It sounds good, but when you take it apart and examine its ingredients you find that they are labeled *masochism* and *chaos*. (It is fruitless to call a Whatter's attention to this, however, as I know from experience. Because they never really listen, they will simply nod sagely and say, "That's what America's all about.")

My most recent Whyer exercise concerns the word *trimester*. How did it become so popular and widespread? It appears only two or three times in the long pregnancy section of *The Merck Manual*; the rest of the text speaks in lay terms of "12 weeks . . . 16 weeks . . . the early months . . . the later months."

Can it be, is it possible, that it reminds our education-worshipping populace of *semester*? Has abortion been subconsciously reduced to a familiar collegiate dilemma? If you drop out of a difficult course in the first trimester, no harm is done and you get your tuition refunded. If you drop out in the second trimester, you lose your money but avoid a failing grade. If you drop out in the third trimester, you forfeit the tuition and get stuck with the failing grade, but you still get out of taking the final exam. Now suppose—

Skip it. Here comes Jesus Christ on rollerskates.

* * *

80

If we insist upon a college on every corner, the least we can do is run them right. The college experience as it now stands exacerbates the battle of the sexes and holds women back in subtle and not-so-subtle ways.

As a student in public high school I used to covet the uniforms of the Sacred Heart Academy girls. Watching them on the streetcar, I thought how simple their lives were. They never had to worry about what to wear; girls with money were indistinguishable from girls like me; and serious girls did not stand out from their peppy classmates because dark blue jumpers and white cotton shirtwaists made everybody look like a grind.

What I was envying was not just the uniforms but the sanity of single-sex education. I still feel the same way: I am against coeducation in secondary school *and* in college.

America's reasons for pushing coeducation have nothing to do with education. Leading the list is fear of prison. What else does a single-sex school resemble? That Americans are obsessed with prisons is evident in the number of prison songs in our folk repertoire. We have talked so much about freedom that we have come to dread anything that symbolizes the lack of it.

Another reason is homophobia. There is a feeling afoot that if males and females haunt each other twenty-four hours a day, nobody will turn queer. It has had the opposite effect: the sexes see far too much of each other and have gotten on each other's nerves. The rise in homosexuality in recent decades has less to do with sex than with rest cures.

Coeducation is the cornerstone of America's self-defeating philosophy of Real Worldism. John Milton called a seat of learning "the olive grove of Academe." Sounds peaceful, doesn't it? Exactly. Americans want our environments to reflect what we call "the real world," sometimes known as "out there." Our fear of being unburdened by pragmatic concerns compels us to turn the educational experience into "real life," the leading ingredient of which is romantic turmoil.

The pro-coed contingent invariably paints itself into a corner with the "sagging enrollments" argument. Saying that girls won't go to a college without boys is to say that many girls still go to college to catch a husband. Saying that boys won't go to a college without girls is to say that boys still want to get laid without driving too far. Nobody dares utter these eternal truths, however, so they talk about sagging enrollments, never realizing that their argument is a strong point in favor of single-sex colleges: they must be the best colleges because MrS. candidates and lazy satyrs don't want to attend them.

Being a pure, or classic, feminist as opposed to the egalitarian kind, my reasons for favoring single-sex colleges are based solely on what is best for *women*, not the gender known as "human beings."

Single-sex schools are safer. Dorm rape, library rape, gym rape are crimes of propinquity that could be eliminated if the mere sight of a male on campus prompted the question, "What's *he* doing here?"

A girls' school cannot have a football team. Because the male football hero presupposes the female cheerleader, coed colleges have a built-in Handmaiden syndrome that no amount of women's studies can topple.

Single-sex schools brave enough to practice discrimination could make female self-esteem a reality instead of the latest buzzword. When Smith College was founded in 1870, their slogan was, "Where the professors are women and the cooks are men." What is the point of a girls' college with male teachers? No woman is truly liberated unless her mask drops before her bosom; if she is taught by too many men she will acquire the habit of classroom dissimulation and never learn to say what she really thinks. Having an all-female faculty, on the other hand, would give bluestockings free rein and a place in the sun, provide more academic jobs for women, and saturate students with the idea of women in authority.

Students at all-girl colleges are never subtly demoralized by fake compliments about their "civilizing influence." This canard, a favorite of male presidents of men's colleges that have decided to go coed, goes like this: "Women are a civilizing influence because they add maturity, hard work, discipline, and a sense of creativity to the campus environment." In other words: "Saved by the love of a good woman." The Victorian female ideal of the angel in the house is still alive and well in the little black hearts of progressive men.

Going to a single-sex school is the only way girls can exercise the power of the old school tie. Egalitarian feminists have condemned this as a male vice but there is no reason why women shouldn't be equally unfair.

Many years ago while working for a temporary help service, I spent several weeks in an office run by a woman who was a Bennington graduate. She was in the process of filling several permanent jobs, and each time the employment agency called she would say in heartfelt tones, "I want a Bennington girl!" By the time I left she had stuffed the place with Bennington girls. Needless to say, it was a strange office, but she had taken care of her own.

Finally, we must not forget the dew on the rose. The moment colleges introduced coed dorms, female fastidiousness came under attack in ways that should surprise no one. This dismal situation was trenchantly described by Lindsay Maracotta in her 1983 novel *Everything We Wanted*:

New rules. This morning when she staggered into the john, there had been some guy in jockey shorts brushing his teeth at one of the sinks. Somebody's date had spent the night. No big deal. Since parietals had been thrown out, there were always men in the dorms; and anyway, modesty was an irrelevant virtue. Still, none of the girls had used the toilet until he was gone—no one wanted to let a boy hear her. . . .

Is there any better way of perpetuating those elementary school battle cries of "Boys stink!" and "Girls are silly!" than letting men overwhelm women's daily physical existence? The sexes need all the help they can get if they are to get along. The old saw was never truer: "Good fences make good neighbors."

A BURNT-OUT
BOOK REVIEWER
CASE

"Get your nose out of that book," Granny used to admonish me. "You'll never get paid for reading."

She was wrong. From 1982 to 1989 I reviewed 265 books and earned a total of $58,034 for reading. These figures come from my impeccably Do Right income tax records but they do not tell the whole story.

It averages out to only thirty-eight books a year, hardly a heavy schedule for one blessed with "inner resources"—the airy-fairy way of saying you love to read. But it did not happen that evenly. My reviewing started the way it does for most writers, as a sideline. For the first year or so I did an occasional review for one newspaper, but then I became what teenagers call popular. Other papers began asking me to review for them, until I had eight calling me regularly. In the final three years my price rose considerably, and in 1987 I signed a contract with *Newsday* for one, later upped to two, reviews a week.

Most of my reviews were clustered in this latter period, which is why I am burned out. Anti-bluestocking Granny's fondest dream has come true: I am sick of reading.

As I look back on my profitable purgatory, certain books stand out as having led to the emergence of my new preferred pastimes, such as defrosting the icebox and learning how to darn really well.

Move over, Anais Nin. In the annals of female neurosis, Marguerite Duras's *Blue Eyes, Black Hair* is the Book of Kells. . . .

I sit here with my face in shadow beside the window opening onto the sea. The sea, the sea, inaccessible, turbulent, crashing. The sea, the sea, murmuring always murmuring, the insomniac sea that licks the sand in the stricken, artless calamity of night.

I have blue eyes and black hair and I am running a temperature in a teapot from trying to cure a homosexual. It all started in a cafe by the sea, the sea, after the beauty of the day had vanished as abruptly as whiskey in a book reviewer's glass. I was sitting with a Jewish Prince from Vancouver who also has blue eyes and black hair. While we were swapping migraine stories at our table by the sea, the sea, the homosexual came in with kohl on his eyes. The prince left and the homosexual started weeping. He was alone and attractive and worn out from watching yachts on the sea, the sea, glide past his body like an infinite caress, so I asked him if he wished he were dead and he said yes.

He sat down and we wept a while, then he made his proposition. Because I looked so much like the Jewish

Prince with blue eyes and black hair, he asked me if I
would move into his room and lie naked on the floor
with a black veil over my face and talk about what it's
like to be tired and cold and despairing by the sea, the
sea. I didn't have anything better to do, so off we went
to our zipless *Weltschmerz*.

The room was empty except for wall-to-wall sheets.
Our relationship was your average existential crisis by
the sea, the sea; I slept, he wept, then we switched.

"I must tell you," he said, "it's as if you were responsible for the thing inside you, that you know nothing of and that terrifies me because it seizes other things
and changes them within itself without seeming to."

"It's true I'm responsible for the astral nature of my
sex," I replied, "its lunar, bloody rhythm. In relation to
you as to the sea."

Most of the time he walked around and around my
supine body and then shrank back against the wall and
wept. I got to like the idea of being repulsive when I
realized how much it was adding to my sense of hopeless
torment. Still, I have to admit that I got a little restless
lying on the floor all day long, talking about being
stricken and knowledgeless beside the sea, the sea, so
one day I went out and picked up a man.

When I got back, the homosexual wanted to hear all
about it, personal things like "his name, his pleasure, his
skin, his member, his mouth, his cries."

That's when I started to worry. Let me tell you, when
you're locked in a room with someone who calls a penis
a "member," you've sunk about as low as you can get.

The female obsession with free-floating nervous conditions that defy diagnosis pervades Joan Baez's memoir
And a Voice To Sing With. As a child, this twelve-string
Agonistes was tormented by a fear of accidentally stepping on ants, but "I was in the practice of pinching the

neighbor's baby," she tells us. "Nervous and excited, I'd give his arm a horrible tweak. . . . Immediately I would begin to feel terrible."

Being nervous and excited and feeling terrible is pretty much what this book is about. Living in Baghdad, Baez came down with such a corrosive case of infectious hepatitis that "the lifeline in my right hand split and disappeared." Back in the States, she suffered from bouts of mysterious anxiety which she describes in prose as clotted as raisins from the box. "Every year, with the first golden chill of fall or the first sudden darkness at suppertime, I am stricken with a deadly melancholy, a sense of hopelessness and doom." When her "demons," as she calls them, hurled her into "nausea and despair," a psychiatrist gave her a Rorschach test in which she identified "myriads of pelvises and skulls," and then curled up on the office floor.

Baez has a spastic colon. The subjects of vomiting and diarrhea are never far from her mind, and her bouts of both are lovingly described. On a plane enroute to a concert in Japan, "I lurched forward and gave a massive retch. Mimi had the flower pot under my chin in a flash . . . No food came up, as there probably wasn't any there." On the day of her wedding to David Harris she entered the church chugalugging a bottle of Kaopectate. During the vows her mind went inexplicably blank when she had to repeat the words "*in sickness and in health*." Silence reigned, and then out it came.

"Oh, shit," she said.

Straightforward sexuality is not Baez's long suit. Looking at the snowflakes on her boyfriend's hair, she wishes she were one of them so she could "melt down through to the roots and then under his skin and just live there"—the best unconscious erotic identification with radioactivity since Phyllis Schlafly announced that the atomic bomb was a gift from God.

* * *

Black Knight, White Knight by Gloria Vanderbilt is her second volume of poor-little-rich-girl memoirs. Her introduction is written in sane, mature English but her narrative voice is that of the seventeen-year-old girl she is recalling. Hence, when she regrets a sexual slip we get: "Please God, I'll go without desserts for a year, forever, if only, please dear God, I'll never as long as I live ask you for another thing, please dear Father God, don't let Phil find out ever, ever, ever."

Engagement to an older man brings on: "It's a BIG SECRET—no one knows it yet except You. And for God's sake DON'T TELL AUNTIE GER. Well—here it is—I'm getting married!!! To Van Heflin!!!!" A seventeen-year-old girl on the phone: "Hello, hello? Oh darling darling darling—Seven, seven, oh darling . . . seven! Yes, it was him and I'm in heaven, but my hair looks hopeless and what'll I wear?"

Flying around with Howard Hughes produces: "Higher in the sunlight, fair blinding, as we topped the clouds . . . Yes! Faster, faster! I called out, as we went higher still." When she announces her wish to marry the conductor Leopold Stokowski, off we go again into deepest froth: "Mummy, Mummy, I said, I'll marry him, live with him, anything he wants as long as we can be together . . . Mummy, Mummy—I love him, don't you understand, please, Mummy, please?"

Faster and faster, higher and higher we go, into a world where red is "crimson," where people "sally" instead of walk. Is Vanderbilt happy? "My heart was like a singing bird." Is she angry? "Blood surged through me." Is she amused? You bet: she puts "ha-ha" in parentheses. Sometimes the joke escapes her, as when she sees a man holding a woman "in smoldering arms." A farewell to arms (ha-ha) said the wicked reviewer.

* * *

The Eight by Katherine Neville is what tactful reviewers call a "busy" novel.

Covering eleven centuries, it is the story of the search for Charlemagne's chess set, known as the "Montglane Service," and the decoding of its ancient curse by a computer jockette named Catherine Velis.

The contemporary story opens in New York in 1972 with Catherine being assigned by her company to set up a communications system for OPEC. Before leaving for Algiers she attends an international chess match at which she meets a sexy Russian grand master named Solarin and witnesses the murder of the British grand master.

The historical story opens with a flashback to Charlemagne's court and then jumps to France in 1790, when the nuns of Montglane Abbey dig up the buried chess set to save it from revolutionaries. The Abbess of Montglane takes Charlemagne's chessboard to Russia on a visit to her girlhood friend, Catherine the Great. The chess pieces are distributed to various nuns, including the novice Mireille, who takes hers to Paris where her guardian, the painter Jacques-Louis David, buries them in his garden while Mireille goes to bed with Talleyrand.

From eavesdropping on legendary historical figures in these fly-on-the-wall scenes, the reader is regularly yanked back to the present to follow the fortunes of Catherine in Algiers where a spy story is unfolding, complete with secret police, kidnappings, and the reappearance of the sexy Russian chess master, Solarin, whom she met in New York.

The idea in all this backing-and-forthing is to create a mystical merge file, so to speak, between Catherine and her eighteenth-century counterpart Mireille, who also ends up in Algeria, where she roams through the Sahara eating whatever her peregrine falcon catches whilst in pursuit of the hot chess pieces and the mystery therein.

This novel should be sold with an attached pencil on a string, like the original crossword puzzle books, so the reader can work out all the codes, anagrams and encrypted messages that keep cropping up. The title comes from—among other things—the fourth day of the fourth month, the birthday that Catherine shares with Charlemagne, and the fact that Catherine and Mireille both have figure-eight marks on their palms. (Mireille got hers from a falcon bite.) The important thing to remember is that eight is the square root of sixty-four, the number of squares on a chessboard. And meanwhile, don't forget what the author said about the relationship between music and math: "It was Pythagoras who discovered that the base of the Western music scale was the octave because a plucked string divided in half would give the same sound exactly eight tones higher than one twice as long."

Back to the contemporary spy story, which by now has dissolved into hopeless babble. In one paragraph alone we get:

> What *was* this formula Hermanold wanted? Who was the woman with the pigeons, and how had she known where Solarin could find me to return my briefcase? What business did Solarin have in New York? If Saul was last seen on a stone slab, how had he wound up in the East River? And finally, what had all this to do with *me*?

I have no idea, but the scene in which Mireille murders Marat in his bathtub and lets her look-alike friend Charlotte Corday go to the guillotine in her place confirms my contention that this is a far, far sillier book than anything I have ever read.

Gabrielle Burton's *Heartbreak Hotel*, winner, unaccountably, of the 1986 Maxwell Perkins Prize, is a feminist geek novel about the comatose visions of a gravely injured, hunchbacked albino named Quasi.

Lying in the intensive care ward bleeding from her hump, Quasi relives her days as a guide at a museum of misogyny, which contains "a Bruges lace tablecloth so exquisitely detailed that young girls lost their eyesight making it." The Male Gynecologists Room contains the "Tiny Town" exhibit named for the doctor who complimented a patient for having the tiniest cervical opening he had ever seen. Other exhibits are the Up Your Ess Room (authoress, poetess), the College of Cardinals Room, the Sears Servicemen Room, and a Menstrual Show in which the menstruals perform in red face.

The Museum's female guides number seven. (Get it? Dwarfs, Deadly Sins.) While Quasi hovers at brain-death's door, the other six guides play out the theater of femininity and its incessant humiliations. Denying the evidence of her senses, a sufferer from chronic diarrhea keeps telling herself that it really is an excellent way to lose weight. Another keeps getting her long hair caught in a shoe-polishing machine but endures cordovan scalp rather than cut off woman's crowning glory. One experiences a masochistic epiphany in Frederick's of Hollywood and longs to die amid the crotchless panties. Another is traumatized for life because teenage boys who hang around the train station are called railroad buffs while girls who do the same thing are called sluts. Still another has never recovered from the sadistic druggist who kept shouting "SPEAK UP, LITTLE

GIRL, I CAN'T HEAR YOU!" when she bought her first box of Kotex.

CAPITAL LETTERS ON NEARLY EVERY PAGE MAKE FOR WEAR AND TEAR ON THE READER. So do sentences that go on for twenty-five lines, sound-effects dialogue ("Ummmmmm ... Ahhhhhhh"), poems, outlines, billboards, bulletins, parables, lists (*e.g.*, every conceivable slang word for the female genitals), the unabridged lyrics of "The Girl That I Marry," and the cutesy, capitalized "Bubblegum Facts" ("BUBBLE-GUM FACT # 77: THERE ARE SOME PEOPLE WHO ARE NOT CONSUMED WITH SELF-CONSCIOUS-NESS EVERY MOMENT OF THEIR LIVES. THESE PEOPLE ARE CALLED MEN.")

Anything else? Yes.

I   object
              to the strange
spacing this author
        uses for
reasons I cannot   fathom.

John Dollar is a novel by Marianne Wiggins, who is now in hiding because she is married to Salman Rushdie. Allah be praised.

Whenever a South Seas castaway novel is plugged with the phrase "veneer of civilization," you know someone is going to be eaten. The Deborah Kerr part in this cannibal saga is played by Charlotte Lewes, a timid, sexually unawakened Englishwoman with one blue eye and one green eye to symbolize her dual nature. When she takes a teaching job in Rangoon, anyone who has ever watched Deborah Kerr molt knows that Tondelayo is in the batter's circle.

Charlotte's transformation from English wren to Bird of Paradise happens in jig time. With no motivation except a change of climate, suddenly she is packing a jade dagger and stabbing a fresh Brit in the hand—"between the fourth and fifth metacarpals," as Wiggins carefully tells us.

Next comes the midnight swim scene—with dolphins.

> She had never seen such sweet expressions. They swam around her, clicking through their smiling beaks, then one dove and came up right beside her. It floated on its back and made clicking noises that sounded like a dozen hollow sticks falling down a flight of stairs, and then it touched her with its flipper on her thigh. A second dolphin swam beneath her, lifting her along its back. She held on to its dorsal fin and let herself be carried and the school, she couldn't tell how many, began a long slow cruise around the lake, displaying Charlotte.

It's hard to say whether the Menstrual Snake scene is fantasy or allegory or what. We *are* in the tropics, so maybe a golden snake really did crawl through the window and bite one of Charlotte's students in the crotch. What I do know is that while these untrammeled English schoolgirls are supposed to be the feminist counterparts of the boys in *Lord of the Flies*, they are actually the Belles of St. Trinian's.

Enter Stewart Granger as John Dollar, an itinerant sailor who shares Charlotte's frantic bed and leads the expedition of colonials who get shipwrecked. Now it's veneer-of-civilization time and Wiggins can get down to the serious business of making us throw up. After watching their pink English fathers turned into white meat at a pygmy barbecue, the girls commit coprophagia with the diners' feces as a way of getting Daddy back. Soon

John Dollar washes ashore with a broken spine, paralyzed and with no one to care for him in his hour of need except the Belles of St. Trinian's, who are hungry again.

In *Titus Andronicus*, Queen Tamora unwittingly eats her slaughtered children in a pie, but at least she got the tenderloin, and at least it was fresh. And at least no one else had eaten it first. Mrs. Rushdie runs a tradewinds version of a greasy spoon flyspecked with pseudo-intellectual hoo-ha ("the symmetry among extremes of one's existence") and gummed up with so many stylistic spills—dashes, crazy spacing, italics, parentheses, marginal notes—that it is almost as hard to read as it is to stomach.

The worst reviewing experience is being disappointed by a book you have looked forward to reading. *Backstairs With "Upstairs, Downstairs"* by Patty Lou Floyd loses its way in a tangle of asides, parenthetical comments, italics, exclamations, far-fetched chapter epigraphs ("What's Hecuba to him, or he to Hecuba?"), archaic language ("thus endeth," "alas," "more anon"), labored poesies about the Muse "sowing daffodil fluff among the petunias," and the author's comparisons of herself to Lazarus coming forth to give us the real behind-the-scenes story, which she never gets around to doing.

By the time I finished it, I was in that snippety-snappety snarling mood that comes over me when I can't get the child-proof cap off the aspirin bottle. If this author wants to talk about Lazarus, she's on. John 11:39 contains an apt appraisal of her book: "Lord, by this time he stinketh, for he hath been dead four days."

I don't know why any editor would assign me an inspirational self-help book, but several have. Book editors are overworked, desperate people. *Betty: A Glad*

Awakening is about how Betty Ford closed the bar and the drugstore and found happiness. After drying out in the Long Beach Naval Hospital she started the Betty Ford Center, which has become her Tara, as much of an addiction in its own way as the bottle or the pill. Long sections on the formation and administration of the Center make the book read like an annual report interspersed with dimestore philosophy. "There's an end to everybody's life, and there is not much we can do about it. A golf ball could come over my roof and hit me on the head while I was out picking roses," she tells us. Knowing Gerald Ford, it could easily happen.

Elizabeth Taylor has had the best vamp lines in the business, as when she challenged prissy Marlon Brando with: "Have you ever been thrashed by a naked woman?" In *Elizabeth Takes Off: On Weight Gain, Weight Loss, Self-Image and Self-Esteem* she says: "Add excitement to low-calorie dishes," "Surprise your taste buds," and tells the story of her wealthy bulimia-afflicted friend whose donations of old clothes arrive at the thrift shop reeking of vomit.

The book is a history of her gluttony, including the finer points ("Bingeing is totally different from the controlled pig-out"). Its style is Late Girl Talk. One day while stepping out of the bathtub, she saw herself in the mirror and she said to herself, she said, "Whoa, great white whale," and went off to the Betty Ford Center. The Center is wonderful, Betty is wonderful, everybody is wonderful in this most upbeat of worlds. Even the tree outside her house is wonderful: "I'm awed by the way it survives and renews itself each spring in a splendid finery of greens and blossoms. Anytime I've wanted to give in to the dark forces in my life—from overeating to self-pity—I look at that tree and find the courage to go on."

Liz backs her readers into the corner with numbing

repetitions of the S-word—self-esteem, self-image, self-worth ("Present your food attractively. If you don't think you're worth it, then you've got trouble with your self-worth")—and delivers pep talks as zesty as oatmeal. "When I make up my mind to do something I have a will of iron," she tells us, and if you don't believe it, ask Debbie Reynolds.

Going from Betty and Liz to deep female intellectuals is the same, only different. *Mysteries of Motion* by Hortense Calisher is a galactic "Grand Hotel" about the colonization of outer space.

As the Pentagon chooses the colonizers of the new planet Habitat, a debate arises about the difference between "average Americans" and "representative Americans." Who will qualify for membership in First Families of Habitat?

If Calisher had stuck to this satire on the elitist underside of the American psyche she would have had a perfect vehicle for a dance of the rapiers, for there is nothing more hierarchical than space technology. From the adolescent pustulents reading about rocket fuel in *Encyclopedia Britannica* commercials, to the beatific astronauts and NASA vicars marking our new liturgical day with the matins and complines of their perpetual countdowns, Black Hole Abbey cries out for a Voltaire.

But no. Just when things are lifting off, Calisher switches to a belles-lettres version of *The Taking of Pelham One-Two-Three* with all the standard action-chase characters: a six-foot-three black woman journalist throbbing with lubricity and soul, a tired businessman, a Jewish survivor of Nazism, and a stowaway.

It still could have been a good read if only the Lit. Crit who once compared Calisher to Proust had kept his mouth shut. She believed him, and so we must slog through a moon shot aimed at Memory Lane. Sentences pulsing with Real Meaning cry out for the sophomore's Magic Marker: "In the constant assemblage of light and dark which is the mind here, even a shoelace he has to bend to becomes part of all capability." How true! The businessman refuses to sleep more than once with any woman because he wants to avoid "the event chains that made up ordinary life." How true! The Jewish survivor, Wolf Lievering, is so overwhelmed by big memories of the Holocaust that he has lost all the little memories of minor hurts and embarrassments that teach us how to be tactful. The people he inadvertently offends flee his presence, which makes him a symbol of isolation, like space. "Your memory is non-Freudian," his psychiatrist explains. "It bears no ordinary grudges."

How true! After his affair with the black woman journalist, whose name is Victoria Oliphant, Lievering changes his name to Jacques Cohen, the name of his late nephew who died in the zoo when an elephant pulled him into its cage and stomped him. A rather large madeleine but a madeleine just the same, though I would just as soon have a plain American Oedipus complex.

The Good Apprentice by Iris Murdoch is about a young man seeking redemption. Edward Baltram, the student protagonist, slips LSD into his roommate's sandwich. The roommate, writhing in ecstasy and moaning that the universe is "a big shaggy scaly fish . . . it's *pingling*," leaps out the window to his death.

Edward goes to visit his father and stepfamily in their country cottage, "a holy place where pure women tend a mystical crippled minotaur"—Murdoch's way of saying that the household consists of three vegetarian feminists and a senile ex-libertine.

We get squeezed in the iron maiden of Murdoch's parentheses: "What young Edward (he was 20) had not expected was that young Sarah (she was 19), who was small and dark and agile like a Russian acrobat, would immediately (how had it happened?) undress him (his clothes had seemed to melt away) and introduced him into her bed. . . ."

Murdoch also indulges in lots of italics to make *sure* we get the *message*. I get it all right; it's called a sick headache. This novel is a big, shaggy, scaly fish that doesn't pingle.

At the Bottom of the River by Jamaica Kincaid reminds me of what Dorothy Parker said just before she died. Asked what she thought of *The New Yorker* of the sixties, she replied: "I don't read *The New Yorker* much these days. It always seems to be the same old story about somebody's childhood in Pakistan."

Jamaica Kincaid is a *New Yorker* writer. The short stories in this eighty-two-page book are about her childhood on Antigua. One passage will suffice to give you the feel of her style and subject matter:

"Standing in front of the fireplace, I try to write my name in the dead ashes with my big toe. I cannot write my name in the dead ashes with my big toe. My big toe, now dirty, I try to clean by rubbing it vigorously on a clean royal-blue rug. The royal-blue rug now has a dark spot, and my big toe has a strong burning sensation. Oh, sensation. I feel—oh, how I feel. I feel, I feel, I feel. I have no words right now for how I feel."

On the edge of your chair? Can't wait to find out what happens next? All right, here's some more.

"In the night, the flowers close up and thicken. The hibiscus flowers, the flamboyant flowers, the bachelor's buttons, the irises, the marigolds, the whitehead-bush flowers, the lilies, the flowers on the daggerbush, the flowers on the soursop tree, the flowers on the sugar-apple tree, the flowers on the mango tree, the flowers on the guava tree, the flowers on the cedar tree, the flowers on the stinking-toe tree, the flowers on the dumps tree, the flowers on the papaw tree, the flowers everywhere close up and thicken. The flowers are vexed."

Go figure.

The so-called "woman's novel" is easy to spot: the protagonists spend most of their time flipping back their hair and deciding that fellatio really isn't so bad if you love him. Sex scenes go on forever—someone is always saying "Tell me what you want" and getting a detailed answer, but the eternal breast-cupping is about as erotic as watching Julia Child construct a pastry cone.

As with so many entries in this genre, *Satisfaction* by Rae Lawrence is about three girls who go to the same college, live in the same dorm, bunk in the same suite, and never, never manage to lose touch with each other after graduation—the plot situation known in blurbese as "their lives entwine." Despite their vastly different troubles (one worries that she is frigid, another worries that she is a nymphomaniac, etc.), they are such interchangeable cardboard cut-outs that the reader keeps seeing fold-over tabs sticking out of their shoulders and knees.

A Glimpse of Stocking by Elizabeth Gage contains enough "hot wetness" to require a dam. It might have had a certain raw pull like *Valley of the Dolls* if only the author had been content to write good bad prose like Jacqueline Susann, but Gage's stabs at bad good prose sound like a cop testifying about "apprehending an individual with a firearm," or a DOS manual written by a nice young Japanese computer expert who is ah-so proud of his English.

"He thought he had seen the last of her. But even the most divergent of trajectories found ways to intersect."

"Where, she wondered for the thousandth time, did

men find this capacity, so foreign to women, of gazing raptly into immaculate climes of moral rectitude even as they trod in a pathetic filth of their own making?"

"Lost in the bedrock, while the fallen leaves, soon to wither into the earth, still lay conscious on its surface, alive with memories, old loves and resentments—and persistent though failing hopes."

The plot is just as bad. Wherever Gage's heroine goes, the long arm of coincidence reaches out to cop a feel. She meets Christine, the dominatrix call girl, when they bump into each other on the street and Christine's bag of tricks spills out whips and ropes onto the sidewalk. She meets screenwriter Damon Rhys when he staggers out of a bar and bumps into her. A few weeks later she goes to a party where, to her utter astonishment, she sees "none other than the man she had bumped into."

A Glimpse of Stocking is 749 pages long, the characters have Cabbage Patch Doll names like Harmon Kurth, Roy Deran, and Buster Guthiel, and it contains this sentence: "Annie was not a burnt-out shell like he." Or like I upon finishing it.

I suspect that female writers are somewhat worse than male ones, but I am in no condition to sort 265 clippings according to pee-pees, so there will be no exact count.

The feminization of America is proceeding at such a dizzying pace that it is becoming harder and harder for men to write like men. Pierre Corneille's advice on choosing themes—"The dignity of tragedy demands some other passion more noble and manly than love"—has in all too many cases been changed to: "My father didn't hug me enough."

The social climate that condemned Robert Bork for

being objective instead of emotional on the bench can hardly fail to have a cultural impact as well. Stephen King hasn't made sense since *The Shining*, Norman Mailer's grandiloquent Egyptian novel makes the *Lear's* horoscope sound Ciceronian, and Ben Stein's *Her Only Sin* is giddy with brand names: "Susan's XJ-6. . . . a young man in a Melendandri blue blazer. . . . her Bottega Veneta briefcase. . . . Sid's silver 450 SL. . . . her Du Pont cigarette lighter." Not even a fire emergency can stop Stein's narrator from looking at labels: "Then I ran back into the beach house and wrote out a note on Susan's Francis-Orr stationery." Stein's characters might not have much depth but they certainly have nice things.

Stein is wise, so wise. "The most haunting of life's mysteries is simply that time, which seems indelible at the moment, passes and is gone," he reveals. His comparisons are unforgettable. Somebody "looked as if he had been dipped in sulphuric acid while his toenails were being pulled out." Hollywood millionaires remind him of "Damascus street assassins in gold and tailored leather, perpetually on guard against a return to dusty souks and goat's cheese."

Jesus wept, and so did I.

In *Lizzie*, Evan Hunter invents a Sapphic revel in which Lizzie Borden is seduced by a British Lesbian whose fustian seduction line would send a real Lesbian flying to the bed of the nearest laconic male.

> "Did our eyes meet, or have I only dreamt it this past month and more? Did I see in your secret gray what was most surely in my revealing green? Oh, your radiant splendor! That fair complexion and dazzling red hair. I wondered in the very first instant—I shall blush myself

now—whether you were tinted so below, and
longed to lift your skirt and petticoats in that
public conveyance. . . ."

This sort of prolix verbosity, much of it in *Cosmopolitan*-style italics, goes on for 159 pages, culminating
in a Lesbian love scene written in a style that teenagers
of thirty years ago called "hot stuff." The word "naked"
is repeated constantly. Lizzie and her companion lie
"shamelessly naked" in "spent passion," exposing their
"pink-tipped globes," the "fullness of their buttocks,"
and of course, their "womanhood." Through it all waves
that grand old flag, the "flicking tongue."

Boomerang by Barry Hannah is a choppy projectile
of pointless puerility. The actual boomerang, bought by
Child Hannah from a comic book ad, is his metaphorical
excuse for the incessant flashbacking and flashforward-
ing in this shapeless autobiographical *ficelle* about growing up in Mississippi.

It contains the usual car trip with reflections on gas
stations, a girl on a gym mattress who takes on a dozen
guys, overreaching stabs at literary style ("the sun comes
up like a purple diamond"), Dick-and-Jane sentences
("The man walks with difficulty. He has a cane. He has
gray hair."), the sophomoric ring of correct politics
("Mississippi College is owned by frowning fat Christians"), frat-rat jokes (a man's beard is a "womb broom"),
and sex scenes that sound like something whispered in
a Times Square movie theater by an old man in a rain-
coat ("She took off her panties and assisted him").

Hannah, who is writer-in-residence at Ole Miss, has
garnered plaudits from Larry McMurtry, Philip Roth,
and Alfred Kazin, but if this is "strong, original writing"
I am Little Mary Sunshine.

Mark Childress's *A World Made of Fire* is set in the rough-and-tumble South of Tom Watson and Leo Frank but it exudes a gauzy timelessness more reminiscent of *Pélleas et Mélisande*. As with all too many Southern novels, the protagonists are children. The two that carry this story are classic stereotypes of the genre: Stella, trembling on the threshold of womanhood, and Jacko, a little boy of the type known in the South as "peculiar."

A "blue baby," Jacko was born dead but miraculously came back to life. After being crippled by polio he survives a fire and gains magical powers. Jacko hexes hunting dogs, makes a horse rear and kill the town doctor, and unnerves people so much (he enters church strapped to a skateboard in lieu of a wheelchair) that he is blamed for a second polio epidemic that strikes the town.

The local Ku Kluxers decide to lynch him, but before they can get at him he is kidnapped by an old black woman named Hoomama, who casts him in the role of unblessed sacrament in her voodoo rite so that he can help her foment a black uprising.

The conversations are written in dialect so thick that reading it is like swimming through grits. We also get mired in descriptive bulletins from the South's leading industry, the ol' factory: the smell of the earth, the smell of smoke, the smell of worms, the dawn smell, the dusk smell, the man smell, the woman smell, and of course the smell of sex, which is "another smell, rich like the earth after rain."

Childress's sentences scream *underline me!*

"The burden of August hung down."

"He carried his hands in his pockets like guns."

"He scraped one long foot on the heel of another, solving an itch."

"The sun felt like milk."

My favorite scene? Having set fire to the wrong house, the Ku Kluxers burn down another that contains a keg of gunpowder. When the explosion rips, the horses, which have presumably been hexed by Jacko, leap ecstatically into the flames with Klansmen attached.

George Garrett's *The Succession* is an historical novel about late Tudor England. Its most striking quality is what rarefied Lit. Crits would call linguistic verisimilitude.

It bee withe a sadd and mournfull hart that I imparte to thee the newes that this bee the worste booke in Christendom. Hast thou ever sat throughe an alehoufe scene in a playe by Will Shakespeare when the dramatis personae saye things like: "Hecuba shalle beard graymalkin 'ere Exeter's jakes the morrow's winkle wends"? And didst thou wonder what the helle was happenyng? That, my burdies, is howe I feele at this pointe in tyme. The lyght is failyng and my breath grows shorte, so bugger full wyll this tale of woe that hath not bosoms nor a Romeo.

At least I never had to review a battle-with-cancer book. An editor did send me one at the height of my burn-out but I sent back with a quotation from Seneca: "*Scorn pain. Either it will go away or you will.*" To my unabashed joy, the editor took offense and removed me from his reviewer list. Got him with a curve ball.

Of the authors I did not review but wish I had, one shines forth as the supreme temptation, so I will review her now. . . .

Welcome to Camp Jejune. The Sublimes are lookin' for a few good novels and I got one right here. *Play It As It Lays* by Joan Didion.

I bet you denouement-diddlers never read it, did you? Yeah, that's what I thought. You look like the kind of blurbheads that wouldn't know an elegiac spiritual wasteland if it jumped up and bit you in the ass. Well, that's gonna change 'cause you're in Book Camp now.

Play It As It Lays is about a girl named Maria Wyeth whose hometown in Nevada has been turned into a missile range. What's that a symbol of? Lemme hear it loud and clear!

"SIR! THE ARID LANDSCAPE OF THE SOUL, SIR!"

Correct! Now, if there's one thing the Sublime Corps won't tolerate, it's the kind of reader who likes a novel to start out good and puts it down if it don't. If I catch you plot-suckers doin' it, I'll turn you into a slice of life quicker'n you can say exposition. Here's how *Play It As It Lays* starts out:

"I never ask about snakes. Why should Shalimar attract kraits. Why should a coral snake need two glands of neurotoxic poison to survive while a king snake, *so similarly marked*, needs none. Where is the Darwinian logic there. You might ask that. I never would, not any more."

All right, story-ballers, whadda we got here?

"SIR! NIHILISM, SIR!"

Correct! Nihilism. Nada. Nothin'. That's what this whole book is about. That's how you separate Sublimes from civilians—nothin' matters to a Sublime but we'll tell you all about it anyway. It's like the *Sublime Corps Manual* says: You gotta read Proust when you have a fever and Joan Didion while you're havin' a miscarriage.

Now back to Maria Wyeth. Her husband's a movie maker. When he stars her in a movie about a girl who gets gang-raped by twelve motorcycle guys, she keeps goin' back to see it over and over again. You know why she likes it so much? Because "the girl on the screen

106

seemed to have a definite knack for controlling her own destiny." Whadda we got? Lemme hear it loud and clear!

"SIR! EXISTENTIAL CHAOS, SIR!"

She starred in another movie where her husband just followed her around New York and shot film: "The picture showed Maria doing a fashion sitting, Maria asleep on a couch at a party. Maria on the telephone arguing with the billing department at Bloomingdale's, Maria cleaning some marijuana with a kitchen strainer, Maria crying on the IRT. At the end she was thrown into negative and looked dead."

All right, Aristotle freaks, whadda you call that?

"SIR! ANOMIE, SIR!"

You bet your ibids it's anomie! It's like her husband says: "Maria has difficulty talking to people with whom she is not sleeping." This is not what civilians call an outgoin' gal. Her and her husband go to this party where she curls up in a ball until he happens to say that he likes to eat breakfast out. Then she sorta comes to and says, real low and to nobody in particular: "In fact he doesn't always get breakfast out. In fact the last time he got breakfast out was on April 17."

All right, McMuffdivers, tell me what her problem is!

"SIR! ALIENATION, SIR!"

When you study the *Sublime Corps Manual* I want you to pay special attention to what the Lit. Crits say about Joan Didion's technique. Here's what General Guy "Blood and Guts" Davenport wrote: "She has given the novel a pace so violent and so powerful that its speed becomes the dominant symbol of her story."

Let's see about that. Listen to this:

"Maria drove the freeway. . . . it was essential (to pause was to throw herself into unspeakable peril) that she be on the freeway by ten o'clock. Not somewhere on Hollywood Boulevard, not on her way to the freeway, but actually on the freeway. If she was not she lost the day's rhythm. . . . an intricate stretch just south of the interchange . . . required a diagonal move across four lanes of traffic. On the afternoon she finally did it without once braking or once losing the beat on the radio she was exhilarated, and that night she slept dreamlessly. . . . So that she would not have to stop for food she kept a hard-boiled egg on the passenger seat of the Corvette. She could shell and eat a hard-boiled egg at seventy miles an hour (crack it on the steering wheel, never mind salt, salt bloats, no matter what happened she remembered her body). . . ."

All right, lube jobs, whadda the Crits call that?

"SIR! A VOYAGE OF SELF-DISCOVERY, SIR!"

Now, lemme tell you about Joan Didion's vision. If anybody drives that much on the L.A. freeway they're gonna run into a lot of smog. That's why Maria's out there, so she can see things without a lot of sharp edges. If Sublimes find a clean window, we blow our breath on it so we can show off our exquisite sensibility! Opaque is where it's at! Heat must shimmer! You gotta have haze! You gotta have refraction! You gotta glimpse everything intermittently through squinted eyes! Squint, you lousy potboilers! *Squint!* Now tell me what you see!

"SIR! AMBIGUITIES, SIR!"

The Sublime Corps has racked up a lot of tributes to Joan Didion, but this one is engraved on the statue of us planting the flag on Pointless View that stands at the main gate of Camp Jejune. It's from Lore Segal's *New York Times* review of *Play It As It Lays*: "Her prose tends to posture like a figure from a decadent period of art, whose fingers curl toward an exposed heart or a draped bosom swelling with suspect emotion."

Whadda you parse-pissin' print lice call that?

"SIR! NEGATIVE CAPABILITY, SIR!"

Correct! Now, *Semper Vortex*, as Sublimes say. Maria Wyeth turns up again in another Joan Didion novel called *A Book of Common Prayer*, only this time her name is Charlotte Douglas. After her daughter gets mixed up with terrorists and disappears, Charlotte goes to a Caribbean island named Boca Grande and waits there for the kid to turn up because Boca Grande is "the very cervix of the world, the place through which a child lost to history must eventually pass."

All right, pudendas, whadda the Sublimes call that? "SIR! METAPHOR, SIR!"

There's another woman on Boca Grande who spends her nights waitin' for her generator to break down so she can recite Matthew Arnold in the dark, so naturally she's impressed by Charlotte's energy. You wanna know about Charlotte's energy? Listen to this:

"I once saw her make the necessary incision in the trachea of an OAS field worker who was choking on a piece of steak at the Jockey Club. A doctor had been called but the OAS man was turning blue. Charlotte did it with a boning knife plunged first in a vat of boiling rice. A few nights later the OAS man caused a scene because Charlotte refused to fellate him on the Caribe terrace, but that, although suggestive of the ambiguous signals Charlotte tended to transmit, is neither here nor there."

Civilians would call that a shaggy dog story but Sublimes have a different name for it. Lemme hear it! "SIR! ILLUMINATING THE HUMAN CONDITION, SIR!"

After that Charlotte spends every day sittin' at the airport havin' hot flashbacks until a revolution closes the airport down and she has to find another place to be a symbol of futility in. Life on Boca Grande gets worse: "The bite of one fly deposits an egg which in its pupal stage causes human flesh to suppurate. The bite of another deposits a larval worm which three years later surfaces on and roams the human eyeball." That's just like Camp Jejune in August—good Sublimes like Joan Didion never forget their Book Camp days.

Finally Charlotte is shot dead in the Boca Grande birth control clinic while she's handin' out rubbers, and her body is shipped back to the States with a red, white, and blue teeshirt draped on the coffin because nobody could find a flag—

Just a minute! I saw that smirk! All right, you cheektonguer, you asked for it. You gonna do fifty op. cits up Hostile Universe Hill before breakfast! That'll learn you to stop lookin' for a laugh in a Sublime book. And in case any of the rest of you funny boys get any ideas, let's go through the drill:

What did Joan Didion say when they asked her who's on first?

"SIR! I KNOW ABOUT FIRST, SIR!"

Who's on first?

"SIR! I NEVER ASK ABOUT FIRST, SIR!"

Who's on first?

"SIR! OTHER PEOPLE ASK THAT BUT I DON'T, SIR!

That's better! Now back to *A Book of Common Prayer.* Didion never gets around to explainin' why Charlotte thought Boca Grande was the cervix of the world, so we gotta turn to the *Sublime Corps Manual* to get a straight answer from the Crits. Here's what Mark Royden "Wild Man" Winchell said: "If it is not altogether clear why Charlotte has come to Boca Grande, it is even less clear why she stays. At one level her insistence on remaining may simply be another indication of her solipsistic innocence."

Well, bookfans, what do you say to that?

"SIR! ON AN OPAQUE DAY YOU CAN SEE FOREVER, SIR!"

Now listen to me, because I'm only going to say this once. There's a certain Crit that Sublimes are sworn to hate, and if I catch you readin' him, I'll cut off your classical unities and eat 'em for breakfast. His name is John Simon and this is what he said about Joan Didion: "After reading such outpourings of hypersensitivity in quotidian conflict, one feels positively relieved to be an insensitive clod."

That's a civilian for you. Now, while you're marchin' to the mess hall for breakfast, I wanna hear the Sublime Corps Hymn loud and clear. Column right, har! Forward, har!

"FROM THE HALLS OF AMBIGUITY
TO THE SHORES OF PSYCHIC VOID!
WE SECURED THE ARID LANDSCAPE
EVERY SENTENCE WAS DESTROYED!
JUST TO FRAGMENT EVERY STORY LINE,
AND TO DROP ANOMIC BOMBS,
WE'LL OBSESS THROUGH SUPPURATING
CLIMES
UNTIL EVERY CRIT SUCCUMBS!"

-IST

John Wayne's last movie was called *The Shootist*. The 1915 Webster's defines the word as *"slang*: one who shoots, esp, marksman." The compilers could not have guessed what Pavlovian reactions their slangy suffix would one day trigger. Were they alive today and back at the task of compiling a dictionary, they would have to create a diphthong, *ageist*, for one who hates old people, to avoid confusion with *agist*: one who hates marbles, esp. shooters.

Above all, they would have to remember that *racist* does not mean one who races, but one who is racially prejudiced, esp. a white one.

In the last few years, race relations in America have entered upon a period of intensified craziness wherein fear of being *called* a racist has so thoroughly overwhelmed fear of *being* a racist that we are in danger of losing sight of the distinction.

Our tension is manifested by the Pop-Out syndrome, wherein company manners stretched to the breaking point produce what is later called an "unfortunate remark." Liberal pundits blame the Reagan administration for creating an "atmosphere" in which such remarks are "acceptable," but Reagan had nothing to do with it. The simple fact is, we're all going nuts.

The most laconic Pop-Out came during ABC's coverage of the 1988 Democratic convention. As the commentators discussed the Jesse Jackson phenomenon, a glum David Brinkley asked, out of the blue: "Is it all over for white males?"

The most flamboyant Pop-Out was uttered by Eugene Dorff, mayor of Kenosha, Wisconsin, on introducing Jesse Jackson: "This country needs a spearchucker, and I think we've got him up on this podium." He later explained that he meant to say "straight-shooter"—and I believe him. The Pop-Out syndrome is like the Search key on a word processor: no matter how far back something is, you can bring it up. When the lifetime contents of Dorff's brain started scrolling, he exchanged a familiar and time-honored American idiom for a word that he obviously had heard in an old racial joke or an old safari movie—"chuck" is British for throw, so I opt for the latter.

At least Brinkley and Dorff were brief. Most Pop-Outs tend to roll brakeless downhill, like Jimmy the Greek's disquisition: "On the plantations, a strong black man was mated with a strong black woman. They were simply bred for physical qualities," he said expansively, going on to extol, with gestures, the big thighs of black men.

Jimmy the Greek was dining in a restaurant and, as he later claimed, didn't realize he was being interviewed. But Al Campanis certainly knew he was on "Nightline" when he said that blacks lack the "necessities" to be base-

ball managers and executives. During the ensuing uproar, Campanis was also criticized for an earlier Pop-
Out that blacks do not make good swimmers because
they are insufficiently "buoyant." Were Americans not
in the throes of a racial nervous breakdown, the buoyancy remark could have served as the focal point of a
salving, empathic discussion about a certain aspect of
slavery that neither jumpy whites nor touchy blacks have
taken the time to analyze and understand.

In *Roots*, Alex Haley mentioned the terror Kunta
Kinte felt on the slave ship when he first saw the ocean
after a lifetime in the interior of Africa. The black novelist Barbara Chase-Riboud goes much further into this
subject in her latest novel, *Echo of Lions*, about the Joseph
Cinqué mutiny of 1838.

> For most of the men, including Sengbe Pieh,
> who had never seen the sea, they had reached
> the end of the earth. Beyond stretched the king-
> dom of spirits, the underworld, and petrifying
> eternity. . . . Seeing it this close inflicted the most
> powerful sensation of terror Sengbe Pieh had
> ever experienced. He squeezed his eyes shut. . . .
> They were going to drown him! They were going
> to send him down into the spirit world at the
> bottom of the sea. He would rather burn, he
> thought.

In other words, water was the Africans' hell. When
they embarked on the Middle Passage, their fear of the
endless ocean probably induced a marine version of ago-
raphobia. This fear was very likely talked about by the
slaves, and the stories passed down to their descendants
in family narratives like the ones Alex Haley grew up
hearing. Is it not possible that many young black athletes
of the present day have been unconsciously affected by

this remote experience? The psychological phenomenon I refer to is called—awkwardly, in this case—"race memory." The young black athlete was raised by parents, who were raised by parents, who were raised by parents who heard their grandparents talk about that terrifying "Big Water." It is not necessary for each generation of a black family to sit down and formally discuss this fear per se, and of course they do not. It is simply that an attitude, however filtered through time, has a way of lingering in the atmosphere and making itself known by a glance, a pause, or words left unsaid, until it fashions a group characteristic.

In all the media explanations, analyses, and hysteria-tinged postmortems of the Campanis buoyancy flap, not one person stopped to think that blacks might take a dim view of aquatic sports for the very best of reasons: water was once connected with their worst terrors and traumatic experiences. This makes common sense to me, but if I went on television and said it I would have to join Jackie Mason in Tasmania.

Committing a racial Pop-Out has replaced farting in church as the nadir of social gracelessness. Just how far whites will go to avoid this occasion of sin was proved last November. Pundits both liberal and conservative were duly shocked after the Virginia gubernatorial and New York City mayoral races, when black Virginian Douglas Wilder and black New Yorker David Dinkins won by razor-thin margins after all the polls showed both winning comfortably. Numerous theories were offered to explain the discrepancy, but the unavoidable truth was that white people lied to pollsters both before and after the election.

"Whites came out of the polling places and lied," gasped University of Virginia political scientist Larry Sabato. "I agree," said Brad Coker of Mason-Dixon Opinion Research. My local paper, the *Fredericksburg*

Free Lance-Star, ventured even further: "Presumably, many whites who voted for [white gubernatorial candidate] Coleman were reluctant to say so in exit polls because they feared they would be viewed as racist."

If a simple *yes* or *no* is risky, what nightmarish possibilities lurk in complete sentences? Fear of commiting a racial Pop-Out is, I submit, one reason why few people speak in complete sentences nowadays. Pop-Outphobia is so widespread that it has thrust white Americans into a perpetual state of tongue-tied incoherence regardless of what subject they are discussing. It is no accident that the racial tension years have also been the years of "-ese" and "-speak," the latest version being what Tom Wicker recently called "Bushspeak."

Herewith the lesser of two feebles on banning semi-automatic rifles:

> But I also want to have—be the president that protects the rights of, of people to, to have arms. And that—so you don't go so far that the legitimate rights on some legislation are, are, you know, impinged on. I am in the mode of being deeply concerned and would like to be a part of finding a national answer.

I am in the mode of being deeply suspicious that the demented ramblings to which we are daily subjected have their origins in the speakers' subconscious dread that they will somehow, some way, blurt out something about race.

Blacks commit Pop-Outs too. D.C. Mayor Marion Barry's frequently manifest an eerie segregationist flavor, as when he called a press conference to reassure tourists and conventioneers that downtown Washington is perfectly safe. The notorious murders, he said, take place in only two of the seven police districts, both poor black neighborhoods east of the Anacostia River. In other words, he called a press conference to announce what I grew up hearing: "It don't matter what they do to each other."

Blacks are free to say just about anything they wish about whites, but craziness reigns here as well.

Alex Haley indulged in some nasty revenge in *Roots* with several observations on the physical repulsiveness of whites. Kunta Kinte compares a white woman's complexion to the underside of a fish, finds offensive the smell of the white seamen on the slave ship, and reflects on "the smallness of their *fotos*."

Barbara Chase-Riboud goes much further in *Echo of Lions*:

> "The color of the Devil. . . . It was the white color that frightened him so—if only they were another color. . . . Obviously if they were to escape he would have to touch one of these men. Could he do it? Could he actually touch something so repulsive? . . . the slit they had for a mouth. . . . the frightening sky eyes. . . . Did the profusion of hair on their bodies mean they were closer to beasts? Were they human beings?

The female figurehead on a ship is a "sky-eyed monstress," a horse's mane is "so much like the hair of white men, I recoil." And of course: "All the faces looked alike to him, he still had trouble distinguishing one white face from another."

This festival of So's Your Old Man suddenly becomes insanely antipodal when Chase-Riboud gets to the description of the novel's "black" heroine, who is the daughter of comfortably-off Connecticut freedmen. After all the racial chauvinism, the author proceeds to paint herself into the corner of the old yellow-is-mellow American "Negro" ideal: "Her pale eyes were like amber set into the face of a bronze statue, her skin only fractionally darker than her mother's olive complexion, as if it had been temporarily darkened by the summer sun."

Another area of black confusion is "Hey, hey, ho, ho, Western Civ has got to go." The chanters comprise the school of black thought that condemns Western civilization as a bastion of white male elitism. At the same time, another school of black thought has claimed for their own several flowers of that very same Western civilization: the Roman playwright Terence, the early Church fathers Cyprian and St. Augustine of Hippo, the Carthaginian general Hannibal, and the Russian poet Pushkin. All, say the claimants, were black.

Moreover, in the area of Eastern Civ, some blacks are now claiming that Ramses II was black.

On March 23, 1989 the *Washington Post* reported the uproar over the Egyptian exhibit at the Texas State Fairgrounds in Dallas. A group calling itself the "Blacology Speaking Committee" threatened to boycott the exhibit unless the organizers changed the pharaoh's image. Said the committee's co-founder, Dallas Jackson: "We are tired of people using our culture and history to make money off us."

He was seconded by Dallas city councilman Al Lipscomb, who opined that more blacks should be involved in the exhibit at the decision-making level, and receive a share of the concessions. Said he: "What we're saying is that the State Fairgrounds are in the womb of the ghetto, in the heart of South Dallas, and [the exhibit] is making mega-millions of dollars. We're saying leave something behind other than being a vacuum cleaner and sucking it all up." In closing, Lipscomb added that it wasn't as if "we're dealing with something from Scandinavia or Ireland, we're dealing with something from Africa."

A hypertensive wail is clearly audible in the response of the Egyptian embassy's cultural affairs director, Abdel-Latif Aboul-Ela: "I wish people would not involve us in this kind of mess, which we have nothing to do with. We are not in any way related to the original black Africans of the Deep South." Ramses II, he said, was neither black nor white but Egyptian. "Egypt, of course, is a country in Africa, but this doesn't mean it belongs to Africa at large. This is an Egyptian heritage, not an African heritage. It really is amazing to claim something like this."

A subdivision of the Civ flaps is the Detroit Symphony flap. David Holmes, a black member of the Michigan state senate, wants more blacks in the symphony, and if he doesn't get them he has threatened to cut off its funding. Senator Holmes is not interested in the musical aspects of the situation: "I have never been to hear the symphony in my life," said he. "I am not going to bore myself just to prove a point."

Tell him that blacks make up only 1.5 percent of the enrollment in classical music studies, and that black students tend to avoid pursuits like classical music lest their peers accuse them of "acting white," and he will doubtless call you an elitist racist (a twofer).

There is no way out of this. Just close your eyes and think of black country-music star Charley Pride, a rugged individualist who ignored warnings of "it's *their* music" and went on to become the pride of Nashville.

Like Senator Holmes, I'll take a raincheck on the symphony, but the question of whether Terence, Hannibal, Cyprian, and Augustine were black is right up my alley, the kind of thing I love to sit up all night and chew over with my fellow Whyers. However, the trouble with such controversies is that they invite the attention of wacko -isters of both races, who will leap at the chance to tie up traffic with a linked-arms march for Pushkin without having the faintest idea who he was, and whose temperaments do not permit them to absorb the fact that educated people have always known that the author of *Eugene Onegin* was the great-grandson of an Abyssinian general.

Such marchers fall into two groups. One consists of self-pitying white feminists of the "woman-as-nigger" persuasion who cut Western Civ on the day the class studied that famous line from Chaucer, "*I am myn owene woman, wel at ese.*" The other group is invariably led by the Reverend Al Sharpton, who can be counted on to announce his discovery of a conspiracy between the French Foreign Legion and the Irish Republican Army to steal all extant copies of *Butler's Lives of the Saints* and paint over Augustine's face with Sno-Pak.

It is becoming increasingly evident that years of -istphobia have robbed Americans of the ability to think straight. The newest bromide, which is proving more popular by the minute, is: "Whites are no longer prejudiced against blacks as blacks; discrimination is now a matter of class rather than race." Where else but America could you banish social guilt by identifying yourself as a snob?

A whiff of Orwellian doublethink comes through in the experiments of black psychologist Darlene Powell-Hopson, who recently repeated the white doll-black doll test given originally by Kenneth B. Clark in 1947. The September 14, 1987 *Time* reported that Hopson found no change; sixty-five percent of black children still preferred white dolls. But. . . .

> After the test, Hopson praised youngsters who chose a black doll and had them recite, "This

is a nice doll . . . We like these dolls the best."
When the preference test was repeated, Hopson
reported a dramatic reversal: two-thirds of the
black children selected a black doll (as did two-
thirds of the whites).

What did she expect? Where is the "dramatic reversal" in emotional bribery and brainwashing? This is an
attack on common sense, yet all too many whites would
accept Hopson's version of the scientific method rather
than risk an -ist by challenging it.

The mental leaps and bounds we take in order to
display correct opinions about race have brought about
the utter collapse of logic. A typical example is an
op-ed from my local paper by Denis Nissim-Sabat, a
psychology professor at Mary Washington College in
Fredericksburg.

His remarks were in response to a column by James
J. Kilpatrick, who defended Arizona Governor Evan
Meacham's controversial recision of the Martin Luther
King Jr. holiday. Kilpatrick stated that King should not
be honored with a national holiday because it puts him
on a par with George Washington, and that we should
wait fifty years until the complete FBI files on King are
available so that we can discover whether he held Com-
munist beliefs.

Taking issue with the George Washington comparison, Nissim-Sabat argued in favor of the holiday be
cause:

> Dr. King has already replaced George Wash-
> ington on the most widely used individual intel-
> ligence test for adults, the Wechsler-Revised.
> There used to be a question on the old test,
> "When is Washington's birthday?" That question

has been deleted and a new question has been added, "Who was Martin Luther King Jr.?"

This is the logical fallacy called *petitio principii*, or "begging the question," an argument that fails to prove anything because it merely takes for granted what it is supposed to prove: because King has replaced George Washington on an IQ test, he should be honored with a national holiday. It is also an example of *ad verecundiam*, or "to the shameful," an appeal to an unsuitable authority, in this case the authors of the IQ test.

Challenging Kilpatrick's suggestion that we wait fifty years to honor King, Nissim-Sabat argues:

> I don't want to have to wait for the 25th anniversary commemorative march on Washington in order to answer my children's question, "Who was Martin Luther King Jr.?" And I don't want them to wait for 50 years before they can tell their children who Martin Luther King Jr. was.

This is an example of *ignoratio elenchi*, or "ignorance of the connection," an argument that overlooks the fact that there is no connection between the premise and the conclusion: no one is stopping this man from telling his children anything he likes whenever he likes. Moreover, it is also an example of *ad misericordiam*, "an appeal to pity."

Next to racist, the worst -ist is *sexist*. Here, our attempt to defy logic and hold correct opinions often leads to the complete disappearance of the subject under discussion: a perfect *reductio ad absurdum*.

The subject of women in the military brings forth

the most sexist Pop-Outs. The standard one is usually some version of what a male cadet said when Virginia Military Institute contemplated going coed: "It'll bust up the camaraderie."

The inchoate emotions roused in men by women's invasion of this most male of turfs were nailed in a lapidarian essay by Donald Davidson in his 1957 book, *Still Rebels, Still Yankees.*

Taking umbrage at the South's worship of the drum majorette, Davidson points out that while nobody can define precisely the function and purpose of these girls, everybody knows what a drum major is. "He is the leader of a band, not in the musical sense, but for purposes of marching and parading. . . . His baton is not merely a frivolous accessory but an instrument of direction with which he marks time and gives signals." Drum majors must therefore be "as tall as possible so as to be better seen and followed, and of a military aspect however ornately uniformed; severity and precision, rather than drollery, [are] the essential thing."

A drum majorette ought logically to be a female drum major. *Ought* and *logic* have nothing to do with it, however, because a female drum major is precisely what she is not:

> When a drum majorette is not so uniformed, is in fact largely without clothes, a new element has entered, and it is time to ask what is happening. When a band is led not by one but by a squad of drum majorettes, all equipped with batons and all equally unclad, you know exactly what is happening. The real function and use of the drum major have been ignored. . . . The drum major has turned into a follies girl, a bathing beauty, a strip-tease dancer. The baton, once used to give commands to the band, becomes the ornament

123

by which the drum majorette attracts attention to her charms. The band, less and less important, gets along the best it can and becomes, in fact, a jazz orchestra accompanying the drum majorette dance.

At this point, what Davidson calls "the rule of abstraction" takes over. The function of the drum major by now has been so abstracted that the abstraction itself becomes the raison d'être for something that is not really happening: non-band leaders are not leading a band.

When, as is often the case, "the band is eliminated entirely and a sound truck substituted," the abstraction grows until the departure from reality is complete: now, non-band leaders are not leading a non-band.

Davidson calls this a "misuse of the ceremony of gallantry." The fear it rouses in men is not merely one of machismo under siege, but a human fear of the loss of basic meaning: the more drum majorettes there are, the more negatives come into play, until the situation dissolves into a meaningless morass of *nons* and *nots* that cancel each other out: *reductio ad absurdum.*

This same rule of abstraction is emerging in churches as they come increasingly under the sway of a radical-feminist version of Christianity. The February 13, 1989 *Newsweek* predicted that the mainline ministry is in danger of becoming another pink-collar ghetto. As more women enter the clergy, "Pay scales go down, prestige goes down and the men get out," according to Diane Spence of the Episcopal Divinity School in Cambridge.

Again, this male flight is not sexism in the narrow sense, but a reaction against meaninglessness, the ultimate theological expression of which came when the Cathedral of St. John the Divine displayed the nearly nude female crucifix called "Christa"—a heavenly drum majorette calling anti-Christian Christians to heretical prayer in a church that became a non-church the moment it committed this blasphemy: *reductio ad absurdum.*

Revulsion against sexual abstraction is beginning to afflict many women and even some feminists. Woman's instinctive view of herself as "the real parent" has been cropping up recently in articles about "nanny envy" and resentment of day-care providers. Women don't want to be abstracted any more than Donald Davidson wants those drum majors to be abstracted. They have begun objecting to the misuse of the ceremony of motherhood.

In a 1989 women's studies book, *Maternal Thinking: Toward a Politics of Peace,* author Sara Ruddick objects to the word "parenting" because she says there is no such thing: it is actually mothering, a female job. Ruddick wants to "protest the myth and practice of Fatherhood and at the same time underline the importance of men undertaking maternal work." That doesn't make a lot of sense, but the subconscious crux of this book seems to be women's growing resentment against the men who are doing what feminists told them to do—fathering, wherein a non-mother takes on the job of parenting, which doesn't really exist: *reductio ad absurdum.*

Thanks to my nightowl habits, I have experienced that unparalleled democratic joy of discovering a new -ist.

Anyone who thinks we have progressed along the road to equality should sit up with me. America is run by a conspiracy of "nightists" who look down on those of us who have a different internal clock.

Watch the three a.m. movie and you will forget all about the movie as soon as the first round of commercials and public service announcements comes on. Prime-time ads flatter viewers with appeals to their middle-class status, but ads for the witching hour assume that no one is watching except sociopathic proletarians and unemployed chronic losers.

"If you or a loved one need a bail bond fast, call Simpatico Sid!"

"Another accident? Another cancelled policy? Don't let your driving record keep you off the road! PWT Insurance can put you behind the wheel again quicker than you can say Poor White Trash!"

"Have you seen any of these individuals? Take a good look at these ten-most-wanted criminals from your area. They might be next door, or at the party you just attended. Call this number. You need not give your name, and you may be helping a friend to help himself."

"My warts almost ruined my life until I heard about Mr. Guy's Seven Days Salon. Now I have nothing to pick but new friends!"

On and on it goes, until the old black-and-white movie gets mixed up with the commercials in your staggered brain. "Heathcliff! Heathcliff! You *can* finish high school!" "Yes, I can be very cruel. I was taught by masters at Blast-A-Bug Exterminator Academy in my spare time."

Nothing is more dependable than American's commitment to equality: you can set your clock by it.

An America without -ists is like an egg without salt, so defenders of the environment and animal-rights advocates are doing their bit to smoke out and hunt down new villains.

The nation's foremost McDonald's-ist is *Washington Post* reader and animal champion Alex Hershaft, who identified the fast-food chain as the Antichrist in a November 11, 1989 letter to the editor:

Acres of forests have been leveled to create pastures and croplands to feed the animals butchered for McDonald's hamburgers and to provide wood pulp for McDonald's packaging materials. The destruction of these forests denies habitats to many animal species, prevents replenishment of groundwater supplies and disrupts our climate. . . . McDonald's is responsible for brutalizing and butchering millions of steers and cows. These feeling, intelligent animals are crowded into huge feedlots, with no shelter from wind, rain or extreme temperatures, until the butcher's knife ends their misery. Hundreds of thousands of native animals are exterminated each year by ranchers raising beef for McDonald's hamburgers, because they are thought to compete with the cattle. . . .

In a November 18, 1989 reply to Hershaft, *Post* letter writer and environmentalist David P. Friedman proves that it takes an -ist to catch an -ist:

Alex Hershaft's letter appears to attack McDonald's but really displays the newest propaganda approach for the animal-rights movement—alignment with mainstream environmentalists in an attempt to gain legitimacy. However, animal-rights supporters fail as environmentalists because they don't understand that truth and logic are important in persuading people to join a cause. . . . What is going on is that Hershaft is screaming about the environment to get our attention and then sneaking in his points about how our society uses animals. . . . Seeing that they cannot make their case on its merits, animal-rights activists are trying to co-opt the en-

vironmental movement. . . . Don't be fooled by
the animal activists in environmentalist clothing.

Environment and animal-rights advocates have acquired a reputation for simplicity, selflessness, and caring, but the more I see of these people, the more I detect
something very different in many of them. The professional environment lover's quest for silence and emp-
tiness and the professional animal lover's hysterical
devotion to anything on four feet hint at the biggest
-ist of all, one that goes beyond race, color, creed, national origin, age, gender, sexual orientation, handicapped status, and previous condition of what-have-you
to encompass a dislike of humanity in general.

A person who dislikes people is sometimes called a
misanthropist but the more common usage is *misanthrope*.
The ranks of misanthropy include Jonathan Swift, Am-
brose Bierce, Henry Adams, and Timon of Athens, who
had *Go Away* carved on his tombstone. Biographer Robert Lewis Taylor identifies his subject as a misanthrope
in *W.C. Fields: His Follies and Fortunes*; in *They Also Ran*,
Irving Stone pins the rose on Thomas E. Dewey. Most
surprising—or perhaps not—is an aging French actress
who has taken up animal rights. In the 1973 book, *Popcorn Venus*, movie historian Marjorie Rosen writes: "Today Bardot, at thirty-eight, seems a peculiar candidate
for a misanthrope, but not long ago she told the French
magazine *L'Express*, 'I hate humanity—I am allergic to
it. . . . I see no one. I don't go out.' "

I am interested in misanthropy and may write a book
about it one of these days because I am a misanthrope
myself. The difference between me and many Greenies
is that I *know* I'm one. The greatest thing we have to
fear in the land of -ist are the people who *think* they are
vessels of love and compassion but really aren't.

They say Tasmania is lovely at this time of year.

TRAD VALS

"This is 'Florence Live in Fredericksburg.' Today we're discussing traditional values. Hello, Boise, you're on the air."

"Am I on the air?"

"Yes, you are. Go ahead, please."

"I just wanna say about traditional values, like, I'm in the loop of thinking, you know, that they made this country in the great mode."

"Thank you, Boise."

Ring up the curtain on another national nightmare. America hasn't been this introspective since "malaise" hit the fan.

Trad Vals are the latest thing; the bee in every bonnet, the buzz in every buzzword, and the fork in every tongue. Trad Vals are what columnists are talking about when they write the ubiquitous op-ed about why the Democratic Party is "not perceived to be in the mainstream." Trad Vals are what get imperiled when amorous politicians go around whispering "Your caucus or mine?" Trad Vals are what Phyllis Schlafly wants to put into school textbooks and feminists want to take out. Tipper Gore is the only person in America able to take notes while listening to hard rock because she will pay any price, bear any burden, in defense of Trad Vals. Lest anyone doubt that Trad Valhood is powerful, remember this: it made Jesse Helms go to an art gallery.

My favorite Trad Vals booster is Goody Two Spikes: Los Angeles Dodgers pitcher Orel Hershiser, who ostentatiously fell to his knees on the mound to thank God for his victory in the 1988 World Series. Since that nationally televised Trad Vals balk, Hershiser has been all over the tube, smiling his kids-are-great smile as he advises, "Eat your Wheaties," and hugging his son while he plugs Johnson's Baby Shampoo.

I don't doubt that he really is this way, I merely want to throw up. Like movies in which Gene Autry strode into a saloon and ordered a glass of milk, this approach implies that traditional values exist solely to set a good example for children. What America needs is someone to set a good example for adults, but we seem unable to moralize without falling headfirst into our usual pedocentric pit.

A matched set of Trad Vals boosters are Mr. and Mrs. American Gothic. Like their namesakes in the Grant Wood painting, they are easy to spot: they are the studio audience members with the urge-to-kill facial expressions that the camera keeps panning during no-holds-barred talk shows.

Why they place themselves in situations certain to upset them is not hard to figure out. They know that when they're in the big city they're supposed to "see a show." This phrase has come down to them from grandparents who remembered vaudeville, so they make a beeline for the only live variety entertainment left.

They manage to pick the most outlandish alternate-lifestyle extravaganzas. If Donahue does a Gay Pride Week show starring the Doting Dads of Dykes barbershop quartet singing "Two Little Girls in Blue," Mr. and Mrs. American Gothic will be there.

If Geraldo features a transsexual guest who explains that he shouldn't go to prison for rape because it happened before he became a woman and got in touch with her true feelings, Mr. and Mrs. American Gothic will be there.

And on that certain future day when Oprah hugs the three-inch jar containing a do-it-yourself extrauterine conception achieved in the privacy of her soundstage, you can bet that Mr. and Mrs. American Gothic will be there with ruptured Trad Vals flying.

But stand by for a surprise. At the end of the show, when Oprah, smiling through her tears, holds up the jar and quavers, "Say bye-bye," Mr. and Mrs. American Gothic will wave on command, because the traditional values of these lipless wonders are easy to subvert: back home, they can be found in their local convenience store, leaning on the counter, lips clamped even tighter than usual, scratching the fifty lottery tickets they just bought.

Mr. and Mrs. American Gothic scare me to death. These are the people who think all writers are Communists, the people who want to ban *Brave New World* because they think Huxley is recommending the life he describes. They think it because they are so goddamn dumb they wouldn't know a satire if they met it in the road. My recurring nightmares in which I am trying to get somewhere or find something are, I believe, a sleep-scrambled version of the waking fear that has lain for years in the back of my mind: that someday during a civil war or a revolution, I will fall into the hands of American Gothics and be unable to make them understand that I am even more conservative than they are. (Should I escape from the American Gothics, I would doubtless fall into the hands of a left-wing contingent led by the feminist editor who called me "Fascist Flossie." Sometimes I wonder why I bother.)

Mr. and Mrs. American Gothic pride themselves on being from Middle America, but the heartland's reputation as the repository of traditional values founders, as far as I am concerned, on a side issue in the Clutter family murders of November 1959. As Truman Capote recounts in *In Cold Blood*, Beverly Clutter, the older daughter who had moved from the family's rural Kansas home some years before the murders that occurred in it, was married in a full-scale white wedding *three days* after the funeral of her parents, brother, and sister. The wedding was celebrated in the same church from which her family had been buried.

The local paper explained: "Vere and Beverly had planned to be married at Christmastime. The invitations were printed and her father had reserved the church for that date. Due to the unexpected tragedy and because of the many relatives being here from distant places, the young couple decided to have their wedding Saturday."

I submit that the young couple and the minister should have been lynched. These drinkless, smokeless, 4-H Club Kansas prigs displayed the traditional values of a frog. They should have postponed their marriage for a year, and the Clutter bride-elect should have used stationery edged in black until she ceased being a Clutter.

Americans are presently longing for high moral standards and the security they bestow, but our love affair with freedom and individualism gets in the way. We are unwilling or unable to see that such standards require a mentality that accepts and derives comfort from iron-clad rules that make no sense, and explanations like "just because." It is a mentality that is by no means limited to unsophisticated provincials, as we can see in this passage about the veil of purdah from Gita Mehta's novel, *Raj*:

> The Maharani could not explain why a piece of cloth woven to such fineness that she could see through it as clearly as she saw through a pane of dusty glass, and which in a breeze clung to the delicate contours of her face, seeming to reveal more than it hid, was the membrane which separated a life of honor from the ways of alien chaos.

Southerners are particularly prone to this kind of thinking. Back in the days of local option, anyone who lived in a Baptist-dominated county that leaped at any excuse to close the liquor stores often found himself rattling a locked door in utter consternation until he noticed the tiny sign containing some such message as: *Closed in honor of William Rufus De Vane King's birthday.*

Who he? The thirsty had to rack their brains or pick someone else's to discover that King was Franklin Pierce's Alabama-born vice president, but instead of getting mad, we experienced a little tendril of satisfaction. There was no earthly reason why we should go parched in honor of this nonentity, except. . . . "It's always been that way," someone would explain.

This "explanation" sufficed. The *always* meshed with the Southerner's definition of general all-round rightness in a way that was as consoling as a drink.

Being a Just Becauser, I have a bent but nonetheless firm commitment to traditional values as I see them.

I am against flag burning. The American flag means

nothing to me except that eleven of its stars represent the Old Confederacy. My motto is, "If at first you don't secede, try, try again." If the South ever does, I would give up my American citizenship without a moment's hesitation and go with her. I regard the U.S. Constitution as Mr. Nice Guy's hankie and democracy as the crude leading the crud. I believe that the First Amendment has sanctified too much barbarism, which is precisely why there needs to be something, like flag burning, that people can't do simply because *it isn't done.*

However, I also believe in being the best of enemies. When Southern cadets withdrew from West Point in 1861, they passed in review before their Northern classmates and exchanged farewell salutes with them as the academy band played "Dixie" in their honor. Enmity without good sportsmanship is inconceivable to me, which is why I have a fantasy of rescuing Old Glory from a pyromaniac and bellowing, "Shoot if you must this old gray head, but spare this Yankee rag!"

I am against sex education in the schools. In the first place, sex is more fun when it's dirty and sinful, which is why the single brief sex scene in *The French Lieutenant's Woman* turned everybody on in a way that Jackie Collins will never be able to match.

Second, children are satisfied with the stork story up to a certain age because the little fartlings are the world's most crustaceous reactionaries; they don't *want* to know, they don't *want* their preconceived opinions toppled. In this period of their lives they are constantly involved with fairy tales, comic books, and extraplanetary cartoons. Magical things are always happening in a child's world, so the idea of a stork (or an angel, or a doctor's bag) being the source of a baby makes sense and ties in with the rest of their fantasy life to produce that feeling of consistency that is the source of all mental health.

Third, if they find out too young what birth control

and abortion are, the egocentricity of early childhood will set them to brooding about whether somebody wanted to prevent or abort *them*.

Finally, Sex Ed is nothing more than another attempt at empire-building by the Educationist Mafia. If every school has a Sex Ed program, lots of Sex Ed teachers and counselors will be needed, which means that teachers' colleges will need more Sex Ed professors and a bigger Sex Ed department, which means that government and foundations will have to give them more money for research, which means that some half-ass diddlysquat will get a patent on a Sex Ed board game (Go to Clitoris).

I favor prayer in the schools even though I come from a family so spiritually lax that as a child I thought "Trinity" meant going to church three times a year.

What used to be called "opening school" is an aid to discipline. Children arrive at school with epiphanies already well under way; the boys punching and shoving and the girls emitting spontaneous shrieks and screams. This was true even in the days when kids walked to school; now that they are cooped up on buses they build up an even bigger head of steam.

A homeroom limited to announcements blasted over a loudspeaker is too much like a pep rally to bring them down. They need a well-defined psychological cutoff point. Ritual and ceremony are calming. I suspect that discipline, rather than religion per se, was the real reason why school prayer was instituted in the first place, and it is still a valid reason for restoring it.

I favor a school prayer amendment to the Constitution. If we got one, what kind of prayer should we adopt? Recommending a religious ritual for American public schools is dangerous business, but as dogcatchers and embalmers say, "Somebody has to do it," so here goes.

"Silent prayer" is a cop-out and "non-sectarian prayer" is an oxymoron, so let's forget about them and use the *prayers* we already have. The three major American faiths are Protestant, Catholic, and Jewish. The school week contains five days. It would be roughly proportional to the distribution of these faiths in America if we reserved the first four days of the week for a Protestant-Catholic-Protestant-Catholic prayer schedule, making Friday, the start of the Jewish sabbath, the day for Jewish prayer.

Heterogeneous school districts in or near big cities contain enough students of all three faiths who could serve as class chaplains. In monolithic areas, school districts could be provided with an ecumenical prayer book containing basic rituals, and the teacher or a student volunteer could stand in for unrepresented faiths.

No one gets excused. We must tolerate each other's religions in America, so let's start doing it at an early age. Atheists who object to all three rituals should reflect on Lord Chesterfield's maxim: "The true individualist has the courage to wear a mask."

The advantages of this plan are several:

1. It would be a microcosm of American society, which ought to please the life-adjustment crowd.

2. The people who want to "put God back in the classroom" would get Him back in triplicate.

3. It allows for a certain amount of common-sense flexibility, *e.g.*, in Utah one of the Protestant days could be Mormon, while in Boston one of them could be Unitarian.

4. It would be educational. If that perennially popular college course, Comparative Religion, can be taught at state-supported universities without causing a constitutional crisis, why can't the public schools profit from a modified version of it?

As a Protestant I have learned the hard way the truth of Mary McCarthy's observation that it is impossible to appreciate much of Western art without a knowledge of the lives of the saints. The Litany of the Virgin is luscious poetry, and the sonorous majesty of the Shema Yisroel rescues "our Judeo-Christian heritage" from platitudinous Reaganese and infuses it with real meaning and historical perspective. If I had children I would much rather they learned a little Hebrew in school than the kind of things they would learn on alternate-lifestyle day in a Sex Ed course.

How would this plan sit with obsessive-compulsive egalitarians? Surely they would leap into the fray demanding equal time for every religion known to mankind and turn my plan into an ecumenical nightmare. Yes, they would try, but people like that got us into the school prayer imbroglio in the first place. We must set limits on such constitutional capers. We can't have kids running around with begging bowls and golden sickles, sacrificing white oxen in homeroom. This kind of esoteric democracy has made millions of Americans furious, and we can't go on indulging it. The three major American faiths are enough—and fair enough.

In my youth, living together without benefit of clergy was called "shacking up." I was against it then and I'm against it now.

Although I was a loose woman in my day, nobody took me for one because I always saw to it that I had my own apartment no matter how slim my income was. I didn't care what God thought but I did care what the mailman thought. I've never seen God and don't expect to, but we see the mailman every day. When we add up the number of such peripheral people who come into our lives it becomes clear that it does indeed matter "what people think."

My sex life began at the tag end of the era that viewed with suspicion women who lived alone, so I took steps to deflect such suspicion. To disarm repairmen and other male strangers who might come into my apartment, I put a crucifix over the bed and a Bible and *The Book of Common Prayer* on the night table. When I lived up North, I added a rosary.

To the male eye, a vanity table strewn with smeary rouge pots and lotions has a whorish aspect. I have never used much make-up, but what little I possessed I hid and left nothing on the bathroom shelf except the virgin's astringent, a bottle of witch hazel. Finally, in the most prominent spot in the living room, I placed a big framed picture of my mother, who shared with Ti-Grace Atkinson a breathtaking ability to pass for a perfect lady until she opened her mouth. No one looking at that picture of Mama would ever dream that her favorite Biblical verse was "*Obadiah tied his ass to a tree and walked thirty leagues,*" so her aura of bogus propriety enhanced mine.

Life for a woman often boils down to little things like this. I suspect that much of today's sexual harassment by landlords, plumbers, electricians, and deliverymen happens because many men read these minor signs and proceed accordingly.

I never had any trouble with such men and I believe it was because I was symbolically respectable. For what it's worth, I believe it was also because I have always been a spit-and-polish housekeeper: a dirty house = a dirty girl. Men are funny that way. I once had a plumber who seemed close to worshipful tears as he told me what a rare pleasure it was to work on such a clean toilet. (For more on this subject, see Lacey Fosburgh's *Closing Time* for a descriptive analysis of the Goodbar victim's filthy apartment.)

I don't believe that unmarried couples have a right to live their own lives "as long as it doesn't hurt somebody else" because *I* am that somebody else.

When too many couples shack up, the sanctity of marriage is destroyed. That's bad for me because I need marriage. Not personally—I would rather be dead than married—but I have sense enough to know that a free-wheeling woman like me could not survive in a society that devalues marriage. Marriage and family stability are the bedrock of civilization and the nucleus of law and order. How could I, a woman completely alone in the world, live by myself in conditions of societal chaos? How could I write in the midst of upheaval? Who buys and reads books when all hell is breaking loose?

If no woman is respectable, how could my prayer-book-and-family-photos ruse work? A woman who lives alone, supports herself, and does what she pleases requires a stable society. I stand four-square behind respectable women because without them I would have no one to imitate.

For purely pragmatic reasons as well, I object to unmarried couples as neighbors and believe landlords should be able to discriminate against them. The need to keep up appearances in life's larger areas keeps people on their toes in small matters. Like anything else that is practiced regularly, respectability becomes a habit. If a couple refuses to get a marriage license, what else will they refuse to do? If they shirk the duties of the married state, what other duties will they shirk? If they choose fun and convenience without commitment, where else will this trait surface?

For starters, check the garbage cans, the parking lot, the hallway, and the elevator.

A minor but irritating offshoot of living in sin is the

way it makes people thoonk. Show me a POSSLQ and I'll show you a thoonker. No, that's not a misprint: I am referring to the socio-psychological undercurrents swirling through the brain of someone in the act of hanging pictures.

Regardless of how trendy they think they are, POSSLQs cannot shake the sense of impermanency inherent in their relationship, so instead of using unequivocal materials like nails and wire they use that bubblegum-like substance marketed as DAP. It must first be softened in the hand and then flattened on the wall, one blob for each corner of the picture: THOONK ... THOONK ... THOONK ... THOONK. About a month later when the DAP dries out and the pictures come crashing down, the whole procedure starts all over again: THOONK ... THOONK ... THOONK ... THOONK.

This goes on for a year or so until the liberated love birds have a fight and one leaves. The following month the remaining one moves out in the middle of the night owing back rent. The landlord scrapes the azure-blue or hot-pink DAP blobs off the wall to repaint the place for the next pair of POSSLQs, who drop off their futon and drive immediately to K-Mart to buy some DAP.

The greatest threat to traditional values is not the decadence of some but the gabbiness of many. Our preference for philosophy by buzzword has turned traditional values into Trad Vals and consigned it to the same plane as flexibility 'n' sensitivity: Flex Sens. Or compassion 'n' supportiveness: Com Sup. Or awareness 'n' wholeness: Ass Hol. We need to shut up and *think* carefully and deeply about what George Bush would call "the values thing" before we reach the stage described by London *Times* columnist Roger Scruton:

For if you go on long enough, if you raise every question and cast doubt on every unexamined answer, you can begin to justify anything. . . . As we look for the cause of our behaviour, so we take attention away from the act itself, fencing it round with excuses, isolating it from judgement and making inaccessible the only ground in which the seeds of morality can be sown: the ground of individual responsibility. Surely it is this habit of explanation . . . which has most effectively "transvalued" our values. [We invite] the destruction of morality by the habit of explaining it.

A corollary of the traditional values debate is the ethics debate.

Unfortunately, a longstanding measure of ethics has been distorted by *Cosmopolitan* and their ilk. The "pencil test" is now a measure of firm bosoms. If a woman cannot hold a pencil under her breasts, they are firm; if the pencil stays put, she has a problem.

I can not only hold the pencil in place, I could write with it if I had to, which means I am old enough to remember when legless World War I veterans sold pencils on the street. The question, "Should you take the pencil?" was a perennially popular delineator of ethical behavior in those days. In the movie *Norma Rae*, the Jewish labor leader from New York uses it to explain the meaning of the Yiddish word *mensch* to the rural Southern girl: an honorable person gave the veteran a dime but refused the pencil.

I witnessed a passion play on this subject when Granny and Mama had their memorable pencil fight outside the Tivoli theater.

Emerging from the movie, we saw a legless former

Doughboy strapped to a skateboard, his stumps encased in padded leather bags. Seeing us, he scooted over, tipped his cap, and held out a can of pencils.

Granny dropped a dime into his plate and waved away his offer of a pencil. She didn't actually say "Keep it, my good man," but her gesture screamed it.

Mama blew up. "Mother!" she bellowed. "You're full of shit!" Marching up to the startled vet, she dropped another dime in his plate and took a pencil from the can.

They argued all the way home. Granny hauled out her full artillery of parables, maxims, and pertinent quotations about Christian charity from the inspirational verse of Edgar Guest, but Mama stated her case in a single, direct sentence. Her furious words will be seared on my memory forever: "If you take the pencil, it makes him a businessman instead of a beggar."

Whichever side people took in this argument, it followed a full circle leading from the dime to the pencil and back around again. By contrast, today's ethical controversies run up against a broken circle in which the prelude of wrongdoing is disconnected from the deed. Being guilty of "bad judgment" is now a sin in and of itself. It is morality's scene stealer, standing alone in all its short-circuited glory, with no before and no after, no cause and no effect, no wheat and no chaff. Suggest that bad judgment leads to a decision that leads to an action, and that it is the *action* that constitutes the moral lapse, and you will find your name at the top of the -ist list.

Did your congressman fuck a Doberman on the steps of the Capitol? He's guilty of bad judgment, not dog-fucking. Who said anything about dog-fucking? Where in the world did you get that idea? Dog-fucking has nothing to do with dog-fucking. It's a question of bad judgment, and if you don't agree, you're not only an -ist, you're a *phobe*.

With this kind of confusion clouding our endless

debates about morality, it is no wonder that personals ads in alternate-lifestyle newspapers read like this:

> Handsome masochist, 28, seeks disciplinarian to tie me up, beat me with cat o'nine tails, dunk me in ice water, ram me with baseball bat, and stick arrows in me for St. Sebastian fantasy. Non-smokers only.

The more immoral we become in big ways, the more puritanical we become in little ways. While stock market manipulators and politicians steal everything that isn't red-hot or nailed down, consider what novelists are doing.

There are no novelists. They've all turned into "investigative reporters" who waste untold hours scrupulously researching the weather report for Vienna on a given day in 1942, or the schedules for the London-to-Dover boat train in 1910, or the exact moment when a certain embankment gave way in the Johnstown flood of 1889, before they will dare write the scenes they have set in these places. The long-accepted practice of "artistic liberty" is now viewed as a fall from professional grace in the race to honor-bright inconsequence.

I was marked as just such a fallen woman during a recent interview when I got into a wrangle with the questioner over the amount of exact truth contained in my memoir, *Confessions of a Failed Southern Lady.*

Very casually I admitted that I had telescoped some time, switched the chronological sequence of certain events, and left out some family members. All of these practices are necessary for the performance of a writer's first duty: telling a good story. Yet to my astonishment, the interviewer recoiled in wide-eyed horror.

"But it's not a novel, it's a memoir," she gasped. "You mean you didn't tell the whole truth?"

"A book is a book," I replied. "Life never arranges itself in a perfectly readable, coherent fashion. A writer has to make it do so in order to keep the reader interested."

I thought that would settle the matter but she persisted until she was grilling me.

"But your mother had a foster sister that you didn't say anything about. Why did you leave her out?"

"Because I didn't need her. She would have added nothing to the main narrative. If you crowd your stage unnecessarily you confuse your readers."

It was clear that my interviewer harbored a desperate need to express righteous indignation about *something*. Contemporary life is a cafeteria of moral turpitude, but the sheer abundance of it all is too exhausting (and in some cases, too protected) to cope with, so she pounced on my standard literary techniques instead.

The brutal diet and exercise regimens of yuppies contain an intriguing hint of ethical crisis. Their ostensible quest for the flawless body recalls fifth-century Christian hermits intent on mortifying the flesh against lust by subsisting on bitter roots and living in caves, or like St. Simon the Stylite, atop tall pillars at the mercy of the elements.

What are the yuppies trying to mortify? What kind of atonement are they pursuing as they alternately starve and run themselves to death? Perhaps, as overachievers in a society devoid of honor, they see and hear and do things at their Ivy League business schools and on Wall Street that they cannot stomach, and so seek moral purity in a trendy version of self-flagellation.

Moral purity has nothing to do with the body. It comes from the sacrifice of the body to a noble cause, such as that pursued by Honoré de Balzac with the aid of his favorite beverage.

The chapter called "Black Coffee" in Stefan Zweig's

biography of the French novelist should be required reading in the ethics courses that schools of business are currently flirting with. In his famous description of Balzac's eighteen-hour work days, Zweig tells us:

> Without coffee he could not work, or at least he could not have worked in the way he did. . . . He rarely allowed anybody else to prepare his coffee since nobody else would have prepared the stimulating poison in such strength and blackness. . . . Coffee was his hashish, and since like every drug it had to be taken in continually stronger doses, he had to swallow more and more of the murderous elixir to keep pace with the increasing strain on his nerves. Of one of his books he said that it had been finished only with the help of "streams of coffee." In 1845, after nearly twenty years of overindulgence, he admitted that his whole organism had been poisoned by incessant recourse to the stimulant and complained that it was growing less and less effective, and that it caused him dreadful pains in the stomach. If his fifty thousand cups of strong coffee (which is the number he is estimated to have drunk by a certain statistician) accelerated the writing of the *Comédie humaine*, they were also responsible for the premature failure of a heart that was originally as sound as a bell. Dr. Nacquart certified as the real cause of his death "an old heart trouble, aggravated by working at night and the use, or rather abuse, of coffee, to which he had to have recourse in order to combat the normal human need for sleep."

The tribute to coffee penned by Balzac himself reads like a warrior's prayer.

Coffee glides down into one's stomach and sets everything in motion. One's ideas advance in columns of route like battalions of the Grande Armée. Memories come up at the double bearing the standards which are to lead the troops into battle. The light cavalry deploys at the gallop. The artillery of logic thunders along with its supply wagons and shells. Brilliant notions join in the combat as sharpshooters. The characters don their costumes, the paper is covered with ink, the battle has begun and ends with an outpouring of black fluid like a real battlefield enveloped in swathes of black smoke from the expended gunpowder.

Short, obese, physically repulsive Balzac, the original Mr. Five-by-Five, was what Oat-Bran America craves: a hero.

AS YE ROE, SO
SHALL YE WADE

There was an abortion in my family that I found out about in my early teens. Sometime around 1910, my grandfather's sister was seduced—or something—and confided in Granny, who was then a young matron. Saying nothing to my grandfather, Granny took Aunt Jane to the family doctor, who gave her an abortion.

According to my mother, he did it because he was madly in love with Granny and would do anything she asked. It was an unrequited love, but even so, the idea of Granny using sex to achieve her ends stunned me so thoroughly that I never did get around to feeling one way or the other about abortion.

That this story was told—and stretched—so freely in our family circle is an indication of the atmosphere I grew up in. At no time during the many retellings did anyone raise the question of the morality of abortion, least of all Granny, whose ego would never permit her to spoil a starring role with a philosophical digression. By the time she got through with the saga, it had sprouted so many melodramatic wings that there was no way my grandfather could have remained unaware of his sister's plight. Aunt Jane "walking the streets" in a snowstorm, midnight poundings on the door, the seducer banished by Granny—all the ingredients of her favorite Gay Nineties songs, "She's More To Be Pitied Than Censured" and "Take Back Your Gold!"—but not a word about the abortion itself.

I would still share my family's blasé attitude on abortion if times were normal, but lately a feeling has come over me that I cannot shake: Molly Yard is such a little old tennis shoe among ladies that anything she says is probably wrong.

It is futile to expect anti-abortion men to state, or even know, whether they have fathered an aborted baby, but anti-abortion women are always asked about their pelvic history, so here—ever so briefly—is mine.

I got my first diaphragm in 1957 by telling the doctor the then-necessary lie that I was engaged to be married. The lie was excellent training in resourcefulness and the diaphragm made further resourcefulness unnecessary. I used it correctly as the doctor had shown me, and I used it every time. I never got pregnant.

I never got married either, which is probably why the diaphragm served me so well. Diaphragms are ideal for the premeditative atmosphere of affairs, especially 1950s adulterous affairs, when every occasion of delirious abandon was necessarily preceded by cryptic phone calls, passed notes, and the kind of precise synchronization of watches found in old RAF movies, when John Loder or Trevor Howard pointed their swagger sticks at a target map and said, "Our chaps are here, the Jerrys are here, and the Froggies are here." No unmarried woman of my generation could possibly forget to insert her diaphragm because these paranoid planning sessions with other women's husbands went on for at least a week.

Having no need for the spontaneity offered by the Pill, I never took it, nor used an interuterine device. Moreover, whenever anything new—the Pill, IUDs, tubal ligation—came on the market, I always seemed to be in one of my Lesbian periods, so the question of exchanging the diaphragm for something more up-to-date was academic.

The four nagging complications of the anti-abortion stance are rape, incest, birth defects, and the life or health of the mother.

Putting myself in each of these positions, my feeling about the first would depend upon what kind of rape it was. Date or acquaintance rape is a phenomenon of the sexual revolution and so foreign to my experience that I can't think of anything to say about it. In my day, when a woman told a man to stop, he stopped. Teasing to the danger point was not my bag; I never saw any reason to go out with a man unless I had already decided to go to bed with him, so except for one or two unusual occasions, I always finished what I started.

Violent rape by a stranger would make me feel that the baby was *his*, not mine. The alienation of the rape would extend to the baby: because I had nothing to do with the rape, the baby had nothing to do with me. Yes, I would want an abortion, and if I didn't get it I would want to throw the baby over a cliff.

But while I was contemplating infanticide, my Whyer side would kick in and cause some thoughts to weave through my mind. Who among us is not a descendant of at least one violent rape? I once discussed this with a

Jewish woman and our off-the-cuff, thumbnail histories of our respective mother countries produced some sobering reflections.

Did every single one of her ancestresses escape those centuries of drunken Cossacks? Surely not. That is probably the real reason why the law of this dispersed and persecuted people is matrilinear; the child of a Jewish woman must be considered Jewish because chances are good that the father might not have been.

And I? The English manage to keep a straight face when they boast that England has never been invaded but I'm sure my ancestresses would have something to say about that. Roman soldiers raped Celtic women, Saxons raped British women, Normans raped Saxon women, Vikings raped a rock pile if they thought there was a snake under it, and Cromwell's soldiers in Ireland went after my paternal grandmother's antecedents in the name of the Lord. Somewhere in all this happenstance horror, I became *me* instead of somebody else.

So would I throw that baby off the cliff? I don't know.

The best way to keep women from having to abort rape-conceived babies is to increase the punishment for rape by placing much of it in the hands of women themselves.

All women should be allowed to own a gun simply by virtue of being female. A woman who prefers to conceal her gun in her handbag should be given a carry permit with no questions asked. A woman who is willing to wear her gun in a holster on the outermost layer of her clothing should be allowed to do so without having to bother with permits of any kind. In all cases it should be understood that an armed woman not only has a right to defend herself, but a responsibility to come to the aid of other women as well. The feminists want sisterhood? Sister, you've got it.

For the woman who gets raped despite these precautions, we should bring back the public whipping post and give her the option of flogging her rapist until . . . her arm gets tired. This would eliminate the need for garrulous and frustrating rape counseling designed to restore a victim's self-esteem. As the Bible tells us, there is a sure-fire way to feel on top of the world: "Revenge is sweet, saith the Lord."

The question of pregnancy resulting from incest arouses my cynicism in this bicentennial year of the French Revolution, which produced the most famous false accusation of incest in history.

Louis Charles, Dauphin of France, had a character defect that was apparent from earliest childhood. A few years before the Revolution, his mother, Marie Antoinette, wrote in an oft-quoted letter to his governess: "He is very indiscreet and is apt to repeat whatever he has heard, and often, without actually wanting to lie, he adds according to his fantasy. It is his biggest fault and one which must be corrected."

In 1793 the leaders of the revolution took the eight-year-old Dauphin from the imprisoned queen and sent him to live with a shoemaker named Simon, who caught him masturbating. To escape punishment, the Dauphin told Simon that his mother, and his aunt, Madame Elizabeth, had taught him to masturbate. Knowing that the Tribunal was looking for evidence that would ruin Marie Antoinette in the eyes of Europe and thus justify her execution, Simon relayed the story to the Jacobin leaders, who grilled the child until he "confessed" to much more than masturbation.

The Jacobins found the Dauphin remarkably easy to coach. Joan Haslip, a recent biographer of Marie Antoinette, describes the scene:

Intimidated by their presence, not daring to contradict himself, the boy repeated the lie, and encouraged by Hébert, went so far as to say that his mother and his aunt had amused themselves by taking him into their beds and watching him perform. Royalist apologists would have us believe that the wretched child had been bullied and beaten by his tormentors who had forced him into telling that terrible lie. But unbiased witnesses claim that he appeared to be quite cheerful and unconcerned, and that he persisted in his lies, even when confronted with his sister and his aunt.

His aunt called him a "little monster," but Marie Antoinette, on the night before her execution, wrote in a letter to Madame Elizabeth: "I know how much my little boy must have made you suffer. Forgive him, my dear sister. Remember how young he is and how easy it is to make a child say whatever one wants, to put words into his mouth he does not understand."

In America, where anything can become a fad, the number of women who are now "remembering" an incestuous contact in their childhoods cannot be entirely unrelated to feminist hammering on the theme of incest in recent years.

So much has been written on this subject that it would fill a feminist anthology called *The Uncle From M.A.N.* In her 1976 book, *Of Woman Born*, Adrienne Rich wrote:

> When a female child is passed from lap to lap so that all the males in the room (father, brother, acquaintance) can get a hard-on, it is the helpless mother standing there and looking on that creates the sense of shame and guilt in the child.

More recently, Kentucky newspaper heiress Sallie Bingham took up the cudgels in her 1989 memoir, *Passion and Prejudice*. A Southern gentlewoman before she became a left-wing feminist, Bingham sidles up to the forbidden topic by means of sly, erudite hints about the awfulness of families in general and her own in particular. She slugs her father with a classical literary brickbat borrowed from the webby House of Atreus—"I remembered *Iphigenia in Aulis* and the sacrifice of the daughter"—and condemns her mother for voting against her in the family's corporate battle, instead of coming to her rescue as Demeter came to the rescue of her daughter Persephone ("Perhaps no daughter is worth a descent into that Hades where women must oppose the men who support and love them").

These references to ancient Greek drama and mythology serve to keep the subject of incest in the reader's subconscious until anti-capitalist Sallie finally gets to the point with a lurid analogy linking Aeschylus and Marx: "No taboo has more dramatic meaning for the families of the very rich, who rarely find that outsiders 'measure up' and so turn, in secret, to their own kind."

Surpassing both Adrienne Rich and Sallie Bingham is a feminist who is such a threat to the Edenic arrangement that she recalls the old childhood rhyming game that left the unwary in pain: "Adam and Eve and Pinch-Me-Tight/Went down to the river to have a fight/When Adam and Eve were swept out of sight/Who was left?"

Andrea Dworkin.

In her 1987 screed, *Intercourse*, she has this to say:

> Incestuous rape is becoming a central paradigm for intercourse in our time. Fathers, uncles, grandfathers, brothers, pimps, pornographers, and the good citizens who are the consumers;

and men, who are, after all, just family, are supposed to slice us up the middle, leaving us in parts on the bed.

I don't deny that incest happens, but I do not believe it happens as often as Dworkin & Company would have us think. They inject it into the abortion debate to paint Pro-Lifers into a corner, and to provide a *ne plus ultra* for the vindictive divorcing woman who wants to ruin her husband for life. That no divorcing husband has accused a hated wife of incest with their son, and that aunts are going scot-free while uncles twist in the wind says something about which sex has incest on the brain these days.

The feminist insistence that incest is already widespread could become a self-fulfilling prophecy. Considering what has happened to several other ancient taboos in recent years, it is naive to suppose that the incest taboo can survive in a liberation-crazed society that has made a taboo of "judgmental" thinking. The revisionists are already at work. Late last year, transsexual Jan (née James) Morris had this to say in her/his new book, *Pleasures of a Tangled Life*: "Actually all the best sex, in my view, aspires to the condition of incest," and "Particularly graceful, it seems to me, is the notion of love in all its forms between brother and sister." Granted, Morris is an idiot, but idiots get a lot of respect in America.

A "Man-Boy Love Association" to promote the acceptance of sex between men and boys has already been formed; a representative appeared on Junior Downey's show last year, along with a copy of the group's magazine. Feminism's rush to expose and punish incest is on a collision course with their rush to create a brave new sexual order. With millions of working mothers leaving unsupervised brothers and sisters alone together in an empty house, we should not be surprised if some of the sibs take a notion to do what they saw on "I, Claudius," and then form a "Caligula and Drusilla Association." Nero and Agrippina will, of course, feel discriminated against and form their own association. Nor will it end there. Once upon a time, unenlightened fathers were notorious for yelling "Put some clothes on!" whenever they saw their teenage daughters in anything less than a burnoose. But today's New Man fathers, fresh from sensitivity lectures, are "accepting" of their daughters' sexuality, so we could end up with an association called "Daughters of Lot."

If you think it can't happen, harken to this. When Minnesota State Representative Phyllis Kahn introduced a bill that would have granted twelve-year-olds the right to vote, she accused her opponents of harboring "adult-supremacist attitudes."

There it is, the dreaded -*ist* that has the power to silence all objections in the land of the free and the home of the brave. Will *incestist* make it to the majors? Anything is possible in a madhouse, even a very small madhouse, and the one I'm talking about stretches from sea to shining sea.

I suspect that much of what is called incest by overwrought accusers is actually incestuous activity—fondling rather than intercourse. We could discourage such behavior if feminists would get their act together on the subject of male sensitivity. If they want men to hug and kiss their children, they ought to stop talking about incest; if they want to keep talking about incest, they ought to stop nagging men to hug and kiss their children. Our present age of enforced touchy-feely is so confused and confusing that a child could easily get the wrong idea and send a male relative to jail merely by telling what she *thought* was the truth.

We could reduce incestuous intercourse if we took bold steps. In a girl who has not attained her full physical

155

growth, intercourse can tear and result in peritonitis. We should pass laws making intercourse or attempted intercourse with a girl under sixteen an automatic charge of attempted murder.

Meanwhile, what of the girl who claims to be pregnant by her father, brother, or uncle? In many instances we don't know whether her accusation is true or not. One day soon we will know; so much work is being done in genetics that there is bound to be an infallible test before long. When that day comes, such an abortion should no longer be a subject of controversy.

Until it comes, we should let hypocrisy work in mysterious ways, its wonders to perform. For both rape and incest victims, an automatic menstrual extraction or a D&C would ease the minds of everyone concerned and satisfy all but the most frothy Pro-Lifers. Wait a week or however long it takes the fertilized egg to enter the womb, or until just before the victim's next period is due, and clean her out in one of these routine procedures.

Neither she nor anyone else will ever know whether she was pregnant or not. It would be comparable to the blank cartridge in one gun of a firing squad. True, the man with the blank cartridge can tell he has it because it makes a gun fire differently, but that does not change the philosophy of the blank cartridge: someone is allowed to be innocent, so all are permitted to hope.

Aborting a defective baby is hard to argue with unless you are a baseball fan. California Angels pitcher Jim Abbott was born with one hand; happily for the Angels, the ace hurler was allowed to live and become an inspiration for sports-minded handicapped youngsters. The sight of a drooling mental defective makes me recoil in disgust, but I am reverent when I watch Abbott switch his glove from stump to hand and back again in the blink of an eye. Where do we draw the line, and who shall draw it? Eleanor Smeal?

I also question the wisdom of basing such decisions on the up-to-date prenatal tests that supposedly reveal fetal handicaps. With all the "human error" around nowadays, how can we be sure that some worthy citizen of the land of E Pluribus Oops did not screw up? Take a sleep-starved lady doctor intent on Having It All, or a lab technician "working on his relationships" instead of paying attention to what he is doing, or a nurse fuming because her husband refuses to help with the housework, or a records clerk thinking about commiting her "out of control" teenage offspring to a mental institution—any of these people could do for prenatal testing what has already been done for airline safety.

Abortion to save the life or health of the mother is the easiest question to answer in a society that goes by the seniority principle of first come, first served. The problem here is that *health* has been stretched to its outermost limits to include the subjective area of mental health. It has come to mean not whether having a baby would make a woman go stark, raving mad, but that it might *upset* her to have one.

In the annals of unwanted pregnancies, William the Conqueror's mother got upset, Horatio Nelson's mother got upset, Alexander Hamilton's mother got upset, but they all managed. So have countless other unwed mothers, and countless more married women who got "caught." My family, like yours, contains at least one of the latter, and wouldn't you know that the unplanned, unwanted baby turned out to be the pick of the litter?

"Health of the mother" all too often means "convenience of the mother." This is the area of that fast-fading virtue, personal responsibility, whose advocates are now

157

accused of "blaming the victim." Some dumb sonofabitch decides to clean his nails with a power screwdriver,
ends up with an infected hand that has to be amputated,
sues the screwdriver company—and wins! His lawyer
invariably claims "debilitating stress, tension, and mental
anguish," and the jury goes along with it. In today's
atmosphere of neurotic compassion, not one person in
that courtroom, including the lawyer for the screwdriver
company, would dare say, "As ye sow, so shall ye reap,"
but it still holds true, never more than in the matter of
abortion as birth control: as ye fuck, madam, as ye fuck.

Abortion's current dominance of the political arena
represents the ultimate feminization of our national life,
one that threatens to destroy what little grasp of American history we have left. If it goes on much longer,
"manifest destiny" will refer to the menstrual cycle,
"fifty-four-forty or fight" will be lost in a welter of trimester counts, and "Oval Office" will take on new meaning.
The abortion debate also threatens to destroy the
legal and medical professions by forcing them to cope
with scientific "progress" that entered the realm of the
ridiculous in last year's embryo-custody case, when the
pot was stirred by ever-dependable Tennessee, land of
the Scopes Monkey Trial, whose license plates ought to
bear the slogan, "The Satire State."
Snow White and the Seven Embryos stars W. C. Fields
and Mae West. Fields, notorious for hating children,
somehow inherits a little jar containing seven very tiny
bundles of joy that he must never let out of his sight.
To get rid of them, he puts them in a jewel box and gets
on a train that he knows is going to be robbed by Mexican
bandits. His seatmate is a madam played by Mae. They
get drunk together and he tells her what is really in the

jewel box. In a sudden burst of regret over her sinful life, Mae saves the embryos from the Mexicans and leaves them on the steps of a convent with a note asking the nuns to give them a good home.

The next day, when the now-sober Mae reads in the newspaper that all seven embryos are female, she promptly reverts to type. Disguising herself as a worthy matron on a charity mission, she gains entrance to the convent and steals the jar containing the embryos, leaving an identical but barren jar in its place. She makes plans to stock her brothel with the embryos, referring to them as her "farm team."

Meanwhile, to keep from going to jail for abandoning the embryos, Fields must find some way to con his way into the convent, where he thinks they still are. After he steals the wrong jar—

You finish it. I invariably reach a point in the abortion debate when I tune out, and it just happened. One reason for this reaction is my aversion to being on any side of anything; the very words *group, team, committee,* and *movement* make me sick to my stomach. If I could figure out some way to be one-hundred-percent against both the Choicers and the Lifers I would do so, because I enjoyed elementary-school recess only when I got to be "The Cheese Stands Alone" in games of Farmer in the Dell.

The other reason has to do with my peerless sophistication. Nobody on either side of the abortion debate can tell me anything because I heard the fetus story to end all fetus stories at the tender age of ten.

Granny used to take me with her when she visited other old ladies in her set so I would learn how to make social calls and converse in a genteel ladylike manner on acceptable subjects of general interest.

The old ladies lived in narrow three-story row houses on those twisty side streets of Washington, and held court in dark parlors crammed with fusty Victorian artifacts and faded photographs of grim relatives staring down from the walls.

One such old lady was a sherry-drinking widow and Daughter of Everything named Mrs. Balderson. Flaubert her no Flauberts, Bovary her no Bovarys, this is her story:

"Did I ever tell you about my sister-in-law's aunt's cousin's best friend Clara who had the tube baby that never got born? She didn't even know she was in the family way 'til one day she felt somethin' go *ping*! in her parts and she knew, *she just knew*, it was a baby that broke through her tube—tube babies ran in her family, you know. Well, she went to the doctor and he told her she wasn't in the family way and that it was all in her mind, but she could feel the poor little unborn baby movin' all through her body. It kept goin' *tap-tap*! here and *tap-tap*! there, like it was tryin' to get her attention, you know what I mean? Like it was tappin' out a message—'let me out, mama, let me out!'

"Well, the tappin' got worse and worse and Clara kept goin' to the doctor, and he kept tellin' her it was all in her mind. Finally, she got so frantic and beside herself that he said he would do an exploratory operation to soothe her fears. So she went to the hospital and they opened her up, and what . . . do . . . you . . . think . . . they . . . found?

"Two teeny-tiny little footprints on her liver! Just as plain as day, two iddy-biddy footprints! The doctor wasn't goin' to tell her about it but the nurse did—they say she got fired and drank herself to death. Well, poor Clara was just haunted after that. She knew, she just *knew* that the baby was floatin' around somewhere inside of her, so as soon as she got on her feet she went to a spiritualist to try to make contact with the poor little thing. There they sat, night after night, goin' *knock-knock!* on the table, but nothin' happened.

"Well, one day the spiritualist told somebody she knew from the carnival, and they asked Clara to be in a sideshow with the hairy lady and the sword swallower, and talk in a little iddy-biddy voice and call it 'The Livin' Unborn Baby!'

"Well, let me tell you! As soon as poor Clara heard that she just went to pieces and they had to put her away. But you know what? Her liver kept goin' *tap-tap!* 'til the day she died—she lived to be ninety-two—and when the undertaker opened her up to embalm her, *there* . . . just as plain as *day* . . . on her *liver* . . . after all those *years* . . . he saw two teeny-tiny little *footprints!*"

THE BATTLE
OF LITTLE BIG
CLIT

I don't mean to imply that there actually is a Sioux Nation Lesbian Caucus, but it wouldn't surprise me a bit in today's atmosphere of politicized homosexuality.

In my 1985 memoir *Confessions of a Failed Southern Lady*, I related a Lesbian affair I had in graduate school at the University of Mississippi in 1958. It made me the darling of radical left-wing females who assumed that I shared their political views merely because I had gone to bed with a woman.

I was invited to speak at a weekend retreat in the Blue Ridge mountains put on by a gang of muff-diving Druids whose flyer said: "Corn-worshipping Festival, Witchcraft Workshop, Automatic Writing Demonstration, Logic-is-Dead Bonfire, Nude Dancing, Vegetarian Cafeteria, Non-Smokers." I returned the flyer with a note across the top: *"It's time you knew I'm a Republican."*

The mailing lists I got on made me nostalgic for the

days when Granny thought that membership in the Daughters of Bilitis implied an interest in genealogy, and their magazine, *The Ladder*, could lie beside a copy of *Home Improvement* and imply nothing but thoroughness.

Those were the days, in the late fifties and early sixties, known as the golden age of the Lesbian original paperback. Superbly well-written by top-pro commercial authors with pen names like Ann Bannon and Vin Packer, these tightly plotted novels featured sexy, down-to-earth Lesbians who resolved their problems with character and common sense.

All that is gone now. The flyer I got from The Crossing Press advertised *Sinking, Stealing*, "a ground-breaking novel about lesbian parenting." The bonus was a set of postcards called "Goddess Assortment" showing women with their hair wrapped around their ankles and stars flying out of their ears.

Tough Dove Books advertised "planetary healing tools from a lesbian perspective." The ad for the lead novel promised "Lesbian Visionary Fantasy ... *and* Magic!" and went on to describe *Womonseed* [sic] by an author who calls herself "Sunlight":

> As the sun goes down on the longest day in 1999, the women and children gather in a meadow to sing their songs and tell their stories—accounts of their origins and journeys to this land, and the growth of their culture. They have found their way to Womonseed from the southern hills, from northern inner cities. New England suburbs, midwestern towns, the fields of California. Emerging from their struggles in the hard realities of the "former world," the women discover their power, inner wisdom, magic, and their love.

The California-based Institute of Lesbian Studies puts out serious non-fiction. *Lesbian Ethics* by Sarah Lucia Hoagland is an excellent argument for keeping Lesbianism furtive so as to cut down on that festival of ecstasy aforethought known as puff copy. What mainstream publishers get when they request "a word from you" is bad enough, but the clit presses get blurbs like this:

> In a time when much of what is written by non-colored women fails to touch me, *Lesbian Ethics* is a politically engaged philosophy I can relate to, can identify with.—Gloria E. Anzaldua

> *Lesbian Ethics* encourages us to experience lesbian culture from the pits of our individual realities to the well of our collective consciousness. A must read for evolving dykes.—Vivienne Louise

> This is a book in which your best friend discusses and argues with you until 3 a.m., and you finally fall asleep delighted to be a lesbian, able to dream "lesbianism, the theory."—Elana Dykewomon [sic]

With the gay rights movement going full tilt and dykes dragging quilts through the streets, I found myself wishing that I had changed the girl in *Confessions* to a man or left out the Ole Miss love affair entirely. The exclusivity of Lesbianism had vanished. What had once borne the flattering name of "the third sex" had been bumped back up to second—or worse, first—by jargon-spewing socialists and Earth Mothers for Jesse baying at the moon.

Around this time, a woman active in the gay rights movement requested an interview with me. I didn't want to do it, but *Reflections in a Jaundiced Eye* was on the stone so I consented for the sake of sales.

She came to my home. We got off to a bad start when I offered her a glass of wine and she said, "May I see the selection first?"

My "selection" consisted of a jug of Inglenook burgundy and a jug of Inglenook chablis. I took her into the kitchen, opened the icebox, and held them up by their handles.

"Er, no, thank you," she said, her mouth twitching in a patronizing little smile.

She took a scotch and soda and I took bourbon and umbrage. How could such a bundle of caring 'n' compassion be so rude? I could almost hear Granny spinning in her grave. If you're in somebody's home and they offer you a glass of gall and wormwood, by God you *drink it.*

The interview began. Our first clash came when I said, quoting from *Reflections*, that the heterosexual majority has always found it easy to think of Lesbians as nice maiden ladies with lots of dogs who live together for reasons of safety and thrift. Therefore, Lesbians don't need the protection of a gay rights movement because they have always gone scot-free in a homophobic world that reserved its ire for gay men.

"Invisible, hmm?" sneered my interviewer.

"You call it invisible, I call it special," I said.

"Do you like being special?"

"Why not? It beats being persecuted, doesn't it?"

She had to agree, but I got the distinct feeling that she felt being persecuted is where it's at. The suggestion that the barbarians were *not* at the gates of Rome seemed to insult her as much as her wine number had insulted me.

The second clash came when I said that I had always found sex with men pleasurable. Somehow this led to a debate about whether or not I was truly liberated. That's when I flared.

"I've never married—isn't that liberated? I've never been pregnant—isn't that liberated? I've never taken money from a man—isn't that liberated? I've never been struck by a man—isn't that liberated?"

By the time the interview was over, all I could think of was Susan Estrich, the left-leaning tower of pissantry who served as Michael Dukakis's campaign manager in the 1988 presidential race. The interviewer set my teeth on edge just as Estrich had. They were cut out of the same piece of cloth, the Tweedledum and Tweedledee of everything I can't stand. I wanted to take my "selection" and shove one bottle up each ass.

America can feminize anything, so it comes as no surprise that we have witnessed the feminization of Lesbianism. The old dykey gruffness is gone, replaced by a masochistic eagerness to "support" gay men in the AIDS crisis by claiming equal susceptibility to the disease for themselves.

We're *not* all in it together by any means, but to masochists, persecution is indeed where it's at; if the barbarians aren't at the gates of Rome, they will go out and find some and escort them to the gates. In today's climate of irrational humanitarianism and prime-time self-pity, Lesbians have been snookered into the old female game of sacrificing themselves for others.

Late in 1988, AP writer Kim I. Mills reported the news that nurturing dykes had been waiting for: two female-to-female AIDS transmission cases that had been written up in current medical journals. The infecting woman in one of the cases was a habitual drug user; the infected woman in the other case was "a dancer from the Philippines" who said she had had Lesbian relations with "women of many nationalities during several years of travel," but claimed that she had never used drugs, never received a blood transfusion, and—despite all that Philippine dancing—had not engaged in sex with men.

Notwithstanding the obvious clues in both of these stories, the American Lesbian community was duly "shaken," writes Mills, and some "have begun advocating radical measures to avoid spreading the deadly illness among themselves."

San Francisco Lesbian editor Susie Bright, who has not the gift of metaphor, stated: "Lesbians have to pull their heads out of the sand and stop thinking that it doesn't happen to them." Bright advocated some radical measures, "ranging from using rubber surgical gloves to wearing dental dams—thin latex squares used in root canals to isolate teeth from saliva or other fluids—as a kind of lesbian condom during oral sex."

I daresay it would work only for women who could keep a straight face, and Susie Bright probably could.

All of this self-immolative me-tooism is beginning to have the effect I predicted in *Reflections*. The March 7, 1988 *Time* contained an article called "Open Season on Gays: AIDS Sparks an Epidemic of Violence Against Homosexuals." All of the victims were men—except one:

> But taking a stand means taking a risk. In Indianapolis, a few weeks after Kathleen Sarris appeared on radio and television talk shows as president of the gay-rights group Justice, Inc., she was raped at gunpoint and beaten unconscious by a man who insisted he would turn her into a heterosexual or kill her.

In the old days when Lesbians suffered the crushing burden of "invisibility," if Sarris's attacker had met her socially and learned of her Lesbianism he would have shrugged and said, "She'll grow out of it" or "What a waste!" and gone on about his business. He would have told himself, like Casanova, that Lesbianism was "a trifling matter," and the next time he had a beer with his buddies he would have proffered his own version of Count de Tilly's opinion quoted by Simone de Beauvoir in *The Second Sex*: "I avow that it is a rivalry which in no way disturbs me; on the contrary, it amuses me and I am immoral enough to laugh at it."

The most telling sign of the new Lesbian masochists is their eagerness to give up both of their beautiful names for the campy *gay*. *Lesbian* and *Sapphic*, proper nouns rooted in antiquity and classical literature, hardly suggest "invisibility" to a reasonably well-educated person. On the contrary, they bestow three thousand years of recognition, are euphonious to an extraordinary degree, and have always been acceptable in polite society. That homosexual men have not been similarly baptized with comparable names such as *Dorian* and *Ganymede* suggests that it is they, not Lesbians, who are invisible because it has never been possible to speak of them without resorting to medical terms or street slurs.

But now Lesbians have meekly adopted *gay* even though it used to mean *prostitute*, and with it has come a form of invisibility guaranteed to make a masochist's toes curl: gay still means *male* homosexual. Numerous books and articles on "gay issues" make no mention of women whatsoever, and the afterthought inherent in the phrase "gay and lesbian task force" seems to relegate Lesbians to the lower-case joys of making coffee for the fellas, just like the chicks in the civil rights and anti-war movements.

The leading unpopular truth of homosexual life is

that gay men and Lesbians don't much like each other. It could hardly be otherwise; each having surrendered prerogatives that the other wants, each views the other as a fool. In a normal country they couldn't bear to be in the same room together but in America they're in the same minority group.

Paradoxically, the far-left slant of organized homosexuality is inimical to both. Gay men and Lesbians traditionally have been elitists insofar as elitism is understood in an observation by the Irish writer Frank O'Connor: "Yet contact itself is the principal danger, for to marry is to submit to the standards of the submerged population, and for the married there is no hope but to pass on the dream of escape to their children."

This kind of elitism surfaces in the testy imperiousness of the intellectual, career-dominated woman who becomes a Lesbian because she simply can't be *bothered* with the burdens and demands of heterosexuality— what de Beauvoir calls the "reconciliation between the active personality and the sexual role." When the atelier beckons, the family room is invariably scorned.

The elitism of gay men is instantly apparent on entering their homes. Most of those I have known would love nothing better than a return to Louis XIV's Versailles. They have "nice things" because they don't have to pay orthodontist bills or school tuition. They hate blue collars, beer, network television, and camper vehicles because these things are the lares and penates of the people who hate homosexuality the most.

They have a gift, intentional or not, for making all women feel low-class by definition. I once spent a weekend in the home of two gay men. They gave me the guest room over which they had labored to achieve a perfection of decor. As I looked around at the delicate fabrics and heavy, expensive lamps, I felt overwhelmed by a sense of *too-muchness*, unpleasantly aware of the subtle cruelty inherent in a hospitality that made guests afraid to move. I had a sudden, disturbing mental picture of a mother and her children occupying the room, breaking things, making messes, filling it with bad smells. I was menstruating that weekend but I would not put my Kotex in the wastebasket in my private bathroom. I wrapped them carefully, put them in my suitcase, and took them back home to dispose of.

A great many Lesbians and gay men still harbor this sort of elitism. Unable to vote conservative because of the religious Right, they vote for radical left-wing liberals whose leveling agenda, if fulfilled, would be repugnant to them.

Ironically, some of the last vestiges of unabashed discrimination are found in gay publications. Lonely-hearts personals always kick off with GWF, GBF, GWM, and GBM to signify the race of the advertiser, sometimes followed by the phrase "wishes to meet same."

Many of the ads in the Lesbian magazine *Visibilities* would be illegal if ERA were part of the Constitution:

"The Highlands" guest house in Bethlehem, New Hampshire, advertises itself as "New England's largest and best all-gay inn."

The Doylestown, Pennsylvania "Springhouse" is "exclusively for discriminating women."

"The Langtry" in San Francisco is designed "with the woman traveller in mind . . . First class accommodations for the woman traveling on business or pleasure."

"Blueberry Ridge" in the Poconos is described as a "Women's Guest House."

And psychotherapist Sandy Chernick, who has offices in Greenwich Village and Forest Hills, boldly advertises her specialities ("relationship problems, eating problems") under the stern heading, *For Women Only*.

As a vigorous supporter of free association I find the foregoing positively refreshing in a country whose unofficial motto is "Be tolerant or I'll sue you," but not all ventures into homosexual exclusivity fare so well. The February 24, 1988 issue of *Newsday* reported the founding of a Lesbian sorority, Lambda Delta Lambda, at UCLA. The university has permitted them to meet on campus, use the school's name, and apply for money from the student activities fund. "According to university rules, however, Lambda Delta Lambda cannot exclude heterosexual women."

It seems to me that Lesbians have changed greatly since I first explored the terrain in my twenties. Tarot cards aside, the most striking new trait I have noticed is a rabid hatred of heterosexual men.

I recently met, and soon had to get rid of, a woman who formed an unlibidinous but nonetheless trying attachment to me. It took the form of drunken phone calls in which she said such things as, "Men all want to die, that's why missiles are shaped like cocks." She said she wished all men could be killed, "except we'd have to keep a few for breeding purposes," and that she liked to fantasize about a world populated with nothing but women, who would love each other and "have peace."

When I told her she sounded like a 1972 consciousness-raising workshop, she tried another tack.

"Men can crush any woman, at any time, if they decide to destroy her."

This, I knew, was a drunk's sly reference to the fact that *Reflections in a Jaundiced Eye* was reviewed almost exclusively by men and received raves from all of them.

As she rambled on in the same vein, I found myself remembering the Lesbian crowd I ran with in North Carolina in the sixties. One Saturday night at somebody's house, the door suddenly opened and a troop of good ole boys shambled in to show our butchy hostess a new fishing rod one of them had just bought. Exclaiming "Hey, man, that's really neat," she went out in the yard with him and practiced casting. The other old boys volunteered to replenish our supply of beer, and I and another dyke went with them, riding in the bed of the pickup with somebody named Bubba and singing "Your Cheatin' Heart." We got back to the house with the beer and the odd-bedfellows party lasted until three in the morning. That was the night I learned how to play poker. The old boys, knowing the hostess was a Lesbian, figured the rest of us were too, but they were not interested in seducing us to show us "what a real man is like," and they clearly were not after lurid vicarious thrills. I have never seen men and women more relaxed together; the word for the kind of fun we had is "camaraderie."

Now, a great many Lesbians have turned into the worst kind of feminists, purveyors of the man-hatred that Betty Friedan tried so hard to eliminate when she launched what she thought would be a solidly mainstream movement. Thanks to the Battle of Little Big Clit, today's Lesbians gather in caucuses, swap childhood-molestation stories, and lock themselves in the bathroom with a turkey baster full of somebody's brother's semen to take a shot at New Age parthonogenesis.

As I look around at today's Sapphic scene, I find myself wondering why I ever got involved with women at all. At one time I enjoyed telling myself that a strong ego is bound to be attracted to its mirror image, but now I believe the reason was something far less flattering: namely, my neurotic thoroughness.

If there were seven or eight sexes, eliminating some of them from my bed would be both sensible and necessary. But there are only two. That being the case, what is the sexual behavior most likely to be indulged in by a woman who keeps going back upstairs to *make sure* she locked the door? A woman who, before she leaves the house, stands in front of the stove and points to each burner, saying aloud, "You are off . . . you are off . . . you are off . . . you are off"? We are talking about a woman who not only saves Twisties but arranges them by length and color; a woman who has a looseleaf binder called *History of My Car* containing every inspection slip, every repair bill, every Shell flimsy receipt for every lube and oil change going back to 1979—in chronological order. A woman, in short, who is so afraid of missing something that she has proofread every page of the manuscript of the book you hold in your hands TWENTY-FOUR GODDAMN TIMES.

Go figure.

Even if the menopause had not put an end to my sexual desire, I would still relinquish the Lesbianism I once embraced. The politicization of pussy has ruined it for me. I don't mind being regarded as perverted and unnatural, but I would *die* if people thought I was a Democrat.

As for the new Lesbian masochists, if they really want to help gay men conquer AIDS, they should revive that old dykey gruffness and bellow out a paraphrase of the ear doctor's famous advice: "DON'T PUT ANYTHING IN YOUR ASS BUT YOUR ELBOW!"

A LAST-MINUTE
ADDITION

I have just finished writing the final version of this book. The manuscript is now in New York, ready to be turned over to the tender mercies of one of those epileptic cretins known as copyeditors. I am mailing this essay to New York today with instructions to add it to the manuscript. I could wait and add it after I get the manuscript back for my final perusal, but by that time I will be so exhausted from writing STET! beside the 867 sentences the cretin changed that I might forget. Besides, it's hard to run a printer from a straitjacket.

Here is the story behind the last-minute addition. A couple of months ago *The American Spectator* asked me to review a book by an author I had already panned twice in *Newsday*. I accepted the assignment with sadistic glee. The review copy was late in arriving, and I finally got it the day after I mailed the final manuscript of *Lump It Or Leave It* to New York.

I wrote the review last night. I don't know whether *The American Spectator* will have the space to use all of it, so I am including it here exactly as written for the purpose of righting a wrong.

LETTERS FROM A WAR ZONE: Writings 1976-1989
by Andrea Dworkin. Dutton: 337 pp. $18.95

reviewed by Florence King

Mothers of book reviewers are famed for advising their young, "If you can't say something nasty, don't say anything at all." Books by feminists usually bring out the dutiful daughter in me. One feminist in particular has always struck me as such a threat to the Edenic arrangement that she calls to mind the childhood rhyming game that left the unwary in pain:

"Adam and Eve and Pinch-Me-Tight/Went down to the river to have a fight/When Adam and Eve were swept out of sight/Who was left?"

Andrea Dworkin.

She is the author of such sanguinary non-fiction works as *Woman Hating; Our Blood: Prophecies and Discourses on Sexual Politics*; and *Intercourse*, an oddly decorous title for a radical feminist, in which she defines the sex act as a "scarring, hurting, jagged edge of pain and grief," and delivers herself of a comparison that ranks as a classic Dworkinism: "Intercourse and women's inequality are like Siamese twins, always in the same place at the same time, pissing in the same pot." She also published a novel, *Ice and Fire*, wherein intercourse becomes "coitus" ("Coitus is the punishment for being a woman"), and a chapter epigraph is taken from Baudelaire: *"Don't look for my heart any more; the beasts have eaten it."*

I panned *Intercourse* and *Ice and Fire* in a dual review in *Newsday* three years ago and fully intended to do another hatchet job on *Letters From a War Zone*. But I can't. As they say in the soaps, I tried, God knows I tried, but once I got into this book I kept running up against an indisputable fact: Andrea Dworkin emerges here as a rock 'em, sock 'em Carrie Nation who has won my admiration and respect.

Letters From a War Zone is an extremely discrete collection of articles and literary criticism written over the past thirteen years. Most of the articles are about Dworkin's work in the anti-obscenity organization, Women Against Pornography, and the "Take Back the Night" marches the group has staged against porn shops and theaters showing "snuff" movies in which women are raped and tortured.

Dworkin's bête noire is the American Civil Liberties Union. Calling them "radical boy lawyers" with "aging penises" who are "afraid that feminists are going to take their dirty pictures away from them," she heaps scorn on their monomaniacal defense of First Amendment guarantees of free speech, and demolishes their fashionable leftist claim that porn is socially redeeming and culturally valuable by pointing out that the days of erotically decorated Grecian urns are over:

"When pornography was in fact writing, etching, or drawing it was possible to consider it something exclusively cultural, something on paper not in life. . . . Since the invention of the camera, any such view of pornography is completely despicable and corrupt. These are real women being tied and hung, gutted and trounced on, whipped and pissed on, gang-banged and hit, penetrated by dangerous objects and animals. . . . Where is the famous *humanist* outcry? . . . an outcry that we might expect if dogs or cats were being treated the same way. . . ."

In a merciless essay, *The ACLU: Bait and Switch*, she tells the story of how she was snookered into joining the organization. In 1975 at the height of the feminist movement, she received an invitation from the ACLU on letterhead studded with the names of prominent women. Although she had earned only $1,679 that year, she sent them a $15 membership fee. Once she had joined, however, the subsequent letters she received were written on stationery containing nothing but male names. Accusing them of the old "bait and switch" scam, she demanded and got her money back.

In the next few years, the ACLU castigated anti-porn feminists for their "contempt for free speech" and rushed to defend pornographers, as well as Nazis and the Ku Klux Klan. "The pornographers give them lots of money," Dworkin says. "The Nazis and the Klan they help on principle. It's their form of charity work. While we feminists piddled around, the ACLU was doing the serious business of defending freedom."

In 1981, still on the ACLU's mailing list, Dworkin received a fund-raising letter signed by none other than Mr. McGoo himself, George McGovern.

"The letter said that the ACLU was fighting the Right, the Moral Majority, the Right to Life Movement, the New Right, and the evangelical Right. . . . Reading it, one could only believe that the passion and purpose of the ACLU was to triumph over the terrible and terrifying Right. And what were the Nazis and the Klan, I asked myself. Chopped liver?"

Dworkin contends that the ACLU doesn't even know the difference between the Right and the Left because it does not know the meaning of distinction.

"It is time for the ACLU to come clean. Its fight is not against the Right in any form, including the Moral Majority or opponents of the Equal Rights Amendment (as Mr. McGovern's letter claims). Its fight is for an absence of distinctions. . . . I am tired of the sophistry of the ACLU and also of its good reputation among progressive people. . . . There is nothing as dangerous as an unembodied principle: no matter what blood flows, the principle comes first. The First Amendment absolutists operate precisely on unembodied principle. . . ."

She also casts a cold eye on the claim of professional Helpists that pornography cures frigidity and impotence and saves marriages. "Pornography is now used in increasing numbers of medical schools and other institutions of higher learning that teach 'human sexuality' . . . its apologists are everywhere." As for the endless academic research about the effects of pornography, Dworkin, who describes herself as a self-educated writer, replies with the horse sense so often found in people who did not go to college: "I am entirely outraged that someone has to study whether hanging a woman from a meat hook causes harm or not."

Dworkin's difficulties in getting articles past editors who abhor censorship are legion. A collegiate Law Review editor who got a lump in his throat whenever he thought about the First Amendment insisted on major changes in a piece she wrote for him, and turned it down when she refused to make them. She then submitted the piece to the anti-censorship *Harvard Women's Law Journal*, who tried to censor it further and eventually forced her to make some compromises. In her assessment of this run-around Dworkin manifests a refreshingly unfeminist dry wit: "Why did I have to run this gauntlet to get this essay into print? Misogyny, stupidity, and the arrogance of children aside, this editing business has gotten out of hand; it has become police work for liberals."

The essay *Pornography Is a Civil Rights Issue* contains her testimony before the Attorney General's Commission on Pornography in 1986, when feminist supporters of the "sexual revolution" and representatives of *Penthouse*, who sat with ACLU lawyers, heckled her as she spoke.

In the stark Q&A duel, undecorated with exposition, she rises to such Boadicean heights of dignity and fighting spirit that a priest on the Commission, the Rev. Bruce Ritter, thanked her for her "extraordinary and very moving testimony."

Challenged on her belief in an organized boycott of pornography, she replied in words that warm the cockles of a right-wing heart:

"I grew up in an era when people were prepared not to eat lettuce, not to eat grapes, not to eat tuna fish under certain circumstances when the tunas weren't being caught the right way. And the reality is that that constituency who went so long without lettuce, who went so long without grapes, consumes pornography and defends pornography.... I am asking you to help the exploited, not the exploiters.... I am asking you as individuals to have the courage, because I think it's what you will need, to actually be willing yourselves to go and cut that woman down and untie her hands and take the gag out of her mouth, and to do something, to risk something, for her freedom."

Dworkin does not seem to realize—or perhaps want to realize—just how conservative she has become. Describing the warm reception she got at a Toronto symposium on porn and media violence, her bemused innocence is almost comical. "The audience was mostly right-wing.... I am happy to say that the audience responded with a very long, loud, standing ovation. I believe that this speech was a breakthrough in reaching right-wing women."

Her opinion of "mainstream" feminism certainly reaches right-wing women—it's the same opinion held by Phyllis Schlafly: "In the United States, there is a feminist establishment, twenty years in the making, media-created and media-controlled, that is fairly corrupt, bought out by the privilege of its own prominence."

The stern purity with which Dworkin views her calling serves as an inspiration to conservative writers in a liberal-dominated industry: "Writers get underneath the agreed-on amenities, the lies a society depends on to maintain the status quo, by becoming ruthless, pursuing the truth in the face of intimidation, not by being compliant or solicitous."

And as for the *eminence grise* that wraps the fish: "I have never been able to publish anything on the op-ed page of *The New York Times*, even though I have been attacked by name and my politics and my work have been denounced editorially so many times over the last decade that I am dizzy from it."

All this is not to say that *Letters From a War Zone* is without fault. One of the early pieces, a 1978 self-interview intended to parody the many self-interviews of Norman Mailer, does not come off. Among other things, it founders on Dworkin's wish that she could go back in time and sleep with George Sand to save her from all those men, and sinks like a stone with the statement, "I wish Bella were King."

Her critique of *Wuthering Heights* veers off into a tortured examination of racism simply because Heathcliff was swarthy and described as a "gypsy brat." A welter of early-feminist psychobabble (dominance, vulnerability, androgynous ideal) obscures what was very likely the simple truth: having been abandoned on the streets of Liverpool, Heathcliff was probably Black Irish like the Brontës themselves.

Dworkin's description of sexual harassment in a snowbound airport in 1978 throbs with feminist obsessiveness: "Most of the bored passengers-to-be are men. As men wait, they drink. The longer they wait, the more they drink. After a few hours, an airport on a stormy day is filled with drunken, cruising men who fix their sloppy attention on the few lone women. . . . Having been followed, harassed, and 'seductively' called dirty names, [by] ready-to-pounce men. . . . [e]xiting from the plane, I was, in the crush, felt up quickly but definitively by one of the men who had been trailing me."

Why is this always happening to radical feminists? It never happened to me, not even back when my weight was twenty pounds lower than my IQ. Now that I've "caught up," as they say in affirmative-action circles, the only thing traveling men want from me is the aisle seat.

She still indulges in occasional Dworkinese: "On the pedestal, immobile like waxen statues, or in the gutter, failed icons mired in shit. . . ." There are enough references to incest for a small monograph called *The Uncle From M.A.N.*, as well as a trite bow to those famous "ancient matriarchies" that came into being in the early 1970s when feminists took up anthropology à go-go and drained Atlantis.

Her continuing attacks on capitalism and her insistence that property rights are somehow at odds with human rights flies in the face of Fisher Ames' dictum: "By securing property, life and liberty can scarcely fail of being secured: where property is safe by rules and principles, there is liberty, for the objects and motives of tyranny are removed." (*I.e.*, if you can't seize property, why bother?) Finally, she persists in the sophomoric spelling of "Amerika" that long ago became one of her trademarks.

Nonetheless, I can't remember when I have been so happy to be wrong about someone. I began reading this book in a spirit of such unabashed prejudice that I was even prepared to blame Andrea Dworkin for the Orioles' loss of the American League East, but now I like her.